MW01169376

Grandfather

A Novel by

Steven Wilkens

Other titles by Steven Wilkens

Transport
The Passage
Essence of Courage
Tattooed Angels
Harvest moon
Nana's Willow
Redemption
The Lost Tribe
The Sword of David
The Tractor
The Long Hot Summer
Charles' Story
Coincidental Journey
Operation Paradox
Happy Oscar the Model A
Having My Say
When it Rains
The Storm

This book is dedicated to:

The late Eugene and Judy Wilkens

For teaching me first, what being a parent is all about. And then showing me how to be a grandparent.

As always there are people that help make writing a novel possible. First and foremost is my lovely Miss Becky. Daughters Chrissy and Brittany. These three women have given me a life worth living and have always been supportive. And there are so many others: Marge, Lana, Beth, Margo, Karen, Rick, Marcy, and Dawn, all encouraging and guiding me when I need it.

Cover photo: Pixabay.com

Grandfather

CHAPTER 1

Jason Wood looked out across the glistening bay from his office. He had just gotten the call that he knew would come, yet it was one he dreaded. He had then called the airport and booked his flight back to Michigan, but the first available was not for another ten hours so he got up from his desk and walked over to the window.

He pondered his life and how much luck had played a role in it. There were bad times for certain, but every time something bad happened, something happened to off-set it. It wasn't always an equal trade, and often when those things happened, life in general was very painful.

From that pain came wisdom, and maybe even more important a special opportunity was also thrown in the deal. To Jason's way of thinking, it was much like driving a car. You have a flat tire on a stormy night and get drenched changing the tire. Then to dry off and warm up, you stop at a sleepy little diner along the road and have the best meal of your life. You never would have stopped there if not for needing to get warm.

As Jason smiled to himself, he thought back over his young life and couldn't even count all the times that when something bad happened, it turned out to be a blessing. One such case was when he applied to Michigan State only to get turned down. Then to be accepted by a little-known college in Olivet, Michigan. It was there that he was placed in a dorm room with John, who would become his best friend.

John's family owned a steel fabricating business that specialized in making obsolete replacement parts for industrial machinery. None of that meant anything to Jason at the time, but after spending that first summer as an apprentice he fell in love with the entire process. He learned so much and as an added benefit he stayed with John's family and grew very close to them. John's dad, Phillip, soon took Jason under his wing and taught him the front end of the business. Working with the customers and driving sales.

The second summer he spent working in the design department. When a part needed to be remanufactured it had to be designed and programmed into a computer program so their automated CNC machines could reproduce the part. It was during that summer that Jason knew his calling and changed his major to industrial engineering.

Changing his major meant that once again he applied to Michigan State. This time it also included a letter from John's dad and a full scholarship. That was eight years ago, and he never regretted a minute of it. The job had its ups and downs, like any job. There were times that the stress level was high, and nothing seemed to go right. Projects took longer than expected and so on. Through it all he had risen through the ranks and was now Vice-President in charge of design.

John had chosen another path. He had wanted no part of the family business and was now an art teacher in Denver.

The only area of life that Jason felt was lacking was the personal side. He had yet to meet the girl of his dreams. He had dated many, but none seemed to fill what he was looking for in a life partner. Maybe, he thought, his standard was too high. He knew he compared every girl he had ever dated to four women that had meant the world to him; his mother, grandmother, his neighbor Issy and of course Bell.

His mother was a tender soul. Soft spoken, caring, and involved with what was happening in his life. Like so many other things in his life, when he tragically lost her at the age of 12, his paternal grandparents took him in. The worst moment in his life had turned into a blessing. Judith Wood, his grandmother, was so nurturing, and loving. She helped him through the worst time in his life and helped him see what little good he could find. In time he became good at spotting the good and found there to be much more of it than bad.

At first Grandfather Denton Wood was an enigma. Very quiet and seemingly aloof. Life had been very hard on him from the start. He grew up in southern Texas as the only child in an abusive home. His family was dirt poor, and he never had decent clothes to wear and was constantly the object of ridicule from his classmates. To survive he had withdrawn into a protective shell and never let anyone in.

When he turned 15, he got an under-the-table job at a motorcycle shop. At first, he just cleaned the floors and polished the bikes. Eventually the owner took the time to teach Denton, (Denny) how to work on the bikes. When he turned 16, he bought his first motorcycle and from that point on spent very little time at home.

At 17, Denny enlisted in the army by forging his parents' signatures. After bootcamp, Denny was sent to Vietnam. While there Denny experienced personal bonding for the first time in his life. It was a horrific year, and he lost several close friends, but given the choice of re-enlisting or going home, he re-enlisted. Near the end of his second tour in Vietnam Denny was seriously wounded and after stays in hospitals in South Korea and Japan he found himself back in the states in an American hospital.

It was at this hospital that he met his future wife, Judy. He had once again withdrawn into that protective shell, and she was the only one that seemed to understand him. She had a way about her that won his trust, and that helped him open up to her.

When he was released from the hospital, he decided to stay in Michigan and try to win her heart. They had dated for a few months before Judy finally asked him if he was just killing time or if he was going to propose to her.

They were married a week later at city hall. He never returned to southern Texas, not even for either of his parents' funerals.

Jason's thoughts were interrupted when Phillip came into the office. As luck would have it, they had been slammed with work orders that had to be worked. Designs and programs had to be made. Two months' worth of work in the shop had come in all at once and for the last two weeks Jason had worked 12 to 18-hour days. He would still be buried under the load if his boss Phillip hadn't jumped in and helped as much as he could. Phillip was like a second dad to Jason and the feelings were mutual.

Phillip was surprised to see Jason lost in thought staring out the window. When Jason turned around, he noticed a bottle of Champaign in Phillip's hand and two glasses in the other.

"You, okay?" Phillip asked. Noticing the blank, but sad expression on Jason's face.

"I have to go back to Michigan." Jason replied with a shrug.

"What's going on?"

"Just got a call that my grandfather is terminal."

"He's the man that raised you?"

"Yes."

"I am so sorry, son." Phillip frowned. "How soon are you leaving?"

"Flight isn't until tonight."

"What time?"

"8:30pm." Jason answered.

Phillip thought a minute. "Okay, take all the time you need there. You go home and pack and I will pick you up around 7pm and drive you to the airport. We're all set here for a few weeks anyway."

"It may take longer than a couple weeks." Jason pointed out.

"Yes, it could." Phillip thought about that for a moment. "Pack your tools and computer for shipping. When you get to Michigan, call me with an address and I'll ship the computer and tools to you. That way you can be where you need to be and still be able to help us out."

"That will work." Jason agreed. "What's the bubbly for?"

"Just wanted to celebrate your hard work over the last couple of weeks."

"Then let's." Jason forced a smile. "It sounds good to me right now."

Phillip set the glasses down and popped the cork. After filling the two glasses and handing one to Jason, he took the other and held it out toward Jason. "To Grandfather."

"To Grandfather." Jason agreed and downed the champagne."

The airport was nearly vacant when Phillip dropped Jason off. Jason was able to check in and proceed to the waiting area in less than ten minutes. His flight wouldn't board for another 40 minutes so he made himself comfortable and soon found himself going back in time in his mind. He remembered the big moment his life changed dramatically.

It was such a normal day in every way. He was up before the sun. Showered and dressed while his mother made breakfast. Dad had already left for work at a distribution center. After breakfast, Jason gathered up his books and put them in his backpack, and silently walked past his mother on his way out the door.

"Are we forgetting something?" His mother asked.

"Mom, I'm not a little kid anymore."

"You'll always be my little kid," she smiled and allowed him out the door without a goodbye kiss.

The two-block walk wasn't far in the warmer months, but during a Michigan December, it was as far as he wanted to walk. He always tried to time it so he wouldn't have to wait long for the bus to arrive, but this morning the bus was late. Probably slick roads as a light snow was falling and the temperature hovered around 20° with a fresh breeze out of the north.

After just a few minutes past its regular time, the bus arrived and the twelve kids that waited at the same stop climbed aboard the chilly, but better than outside the school bus. All his classes that day went by without being memorable. Lunch was lunch, he sat with the same kids as always and then rode the same bus back home after school. From that point on things changed in a big, horrible way.

The driveway was covered in fresh snow with evidence of his dad's SUV having come home and then left again. There were partially snowed in footprints of his father going from the SUV to the back door. Then another partially covered set of smaller prints showing where his mother had returned to the SUV with dad, and then left. Inside the backdoor on the counter was a note from mom asking him to shovel the drive and walk. His mother had a late afternoon doctor's appointment, and her car wasn't very good in the snow, so his dad decided it would be best if they took his truck.

It took him about an hour to shovel both the drive and the walks, and by then the winter sky was getting dark. He went inside, took his coat and boots off, made himself a cup of hot cocoa and started in on his homework. Most of that went quickly until he started on the history assignment. History always fascinated Jason, and the Civil War was always of great interest. The assignment was to write a report on the battle of Shiloh, and Jason was soon lost in his research and lost all track of time until a knock at the door snapped him out of it.

He was surprised to find his Grandparents on his father's side standing at the door. Grandfather wore a grim expression that Jason thought nothing of, since Grandfather never seemed to smile much and was a man of very few words, or so the case had always been with him. Grandmother looked sad, or worried and told Jason to grab his coat and come with them. Why? Jason didn't ask and they didn't say, at least until they were in Grandfather's old car and racing down slippery streets and almost wrecking a couple of times.

"What's wrong?" Jason quietly asked.

"There's been an accident," Grandfather replied without a hint of emotion, but Jason thought he caught a glimpse of moisture around grandfather's eyes.

"What kind of accident?" Jason asked.

"A car accident." Grandmother replied, and then added that Jason's parents had been taken to the hospital.

At the hospital Jason's world came apart. His father had already passed, his mother was in emergency surgery. A doctor quietly talked to the

Grandparents for a moment and then lead them to the elevator.

The three of them took the elevator up to the third floor and turned right following the signs toward the surgical wing. They stopped at the Nurses' station and were directed to a waiting room at the end of the hall. An hour passed before a doctor came in and explained that there had been just too much damage.

After another twenty minutes they were allowed to see both of Jason's parents' bodies. By this time Jason was in a daze. None of this should be happening. He should be home, with his parents having dinner. Tears fell to be sure, but the fog that enshrouded his mind and heart left him too numb to react as his heart felt.

Grandfather was basically in the same boat, like he was on autopilot, Grandmother had wrapped her arm around Jason and hadn't let go. When they left the hospital very little was said, other than they would go back to Jason's house so he could get a few clothes and toiletries that he would need for a few days. Grandfather stayed in the car while Grandmother walked into the house with Jason but remained at the back door as Jason went about gathering up the items, he thought he would need. It wasn't until they were about to walk out of the house that Jason thought about that morning. He had left without giving his mother a hug and a kiss. They had always hugged and kissed whenever he left for school when he was younger, but when he turned 12 last summer, he felt that he was too old to be loved upon by his mother. That pressed on his mind all the way to the car, but it wasn't until he had buckled in that he broke down and really cried. Grandfather stopped the car so Grandmother could get out of the front seat and climb into the back seat with Jason. She held him tightly all the way to their house.

"I left this morning without a hug, a kiss, or even saying goodbye," Jason lamented.

Grandfather just glanced up in the rearview mirror while grandmother hugged him even tighter and began crying herself.

When they arrived at his grandparents' home, he was shown to the room that had been his dad's when he grew up there. Some of his father's old keepsakes were still on display. Jason slowly walked around the room and took it all in as if it was the first-time, he had ever seen it. It wasn't. He had stayed in this very room dozens of times while spending the night with his grandparents.

It was, however, the first time he looked upon his father's things, realizing that those items and his memories were all he had left. After walking around the room and looking at and touching his father's keepsakes, Jason sadly sat down on the edge of the bed and tried to come to terms with all that had just happened. It just didn't seem real. It couldn't be. How could it be possible that he would never see his dad's smile or hear his laughter. Or have his mother do all of the million and one things she did everyday that he had never thought of before.

Simple things like telling him how handsome he looked, or spit polishing his face when she felt he missed a spot. Reminding him repeatedly to do the things he should have done on his own. Scolding him for not taking his shoes off at the door. He could hear her in his mind saying things like "sometimes I wonder where your head is at?"

Sitting there with all these thoughts and emotions, Jason lost track of time. It wasn't until Grandfather knocked on the door and told him that grandma had food on the table.

When Jason got to the kitchen Grandma had the food on the table and was just waiting for him to take a seat. As soon as Jason sat down, she turned to grandpa and asked him to say grace.

"I'd rather not." Came his surprising reply.

Grandma just sadly looked at her husband and then with a sad smile asked if Jason would be so kind as to honor them with a blessing. Jason bowed his head and started by asking God to tenderly accept his parents in his loving arms. It was as far as he got before breaking down. Grandma said "Amen" as she patted his hand lovingly.

The meal was a very quiet affair. No one knew what to say, so they ate in silence. After eating, Jason helped with the dishes, which made his grandmother smile. At bedtime, she walked him to his room and sat on the edge of the bed. They talked a little, nothing of real importance, other than she told him that they had to go to the funeral home in the morning to make the arrangements. She asked if he would like to go along? He simply nodded that he did.

She smiled a sad smile, brushed his hair off his forehead and then tucked him in. On her way out of the room, she turned the light off and closed the door.

For the next hour or so, Jason lay there in the dark thinking of his parents. So many things he wished he could tell them. More than any of that, he so deeply wanted to hug his mother, kiss her cheek, and tell her that he loved her. As he should have done that morning.

Jason had fallen asleep for a time, just how long, he didn't know. At first, he wasn't sure of what had awakened him. Then he heard it, a muffled sound of Grandmother crying. Without thought, Jason got out of bed and slowly made his way to the living room. His Grandparents were sitting on the sofa with photo albums opened on the coffee table before them. Grandfather was holding Grandmother in his big arms as she cried her heart out. Jason stopped at the edge of the room and just watched and listened.

Between bouts of anguish Grandmother was saying something, but

Jason couldn't make it out. Tears began falling from his own eyes as well. He turned back around and returned to the bedroom. Instead of getting back into bed, he knelt at the side of it and prayed. He prayed for his lost parents, and he prayed for his grandparents. He also prayed for strength to help them get through this horrible nightmare as best they could.

During the night, he drifted off to sleep several times, but never for very long. His dreams broke his heart, and Grandmother could still be heard crying and talking from the other room. Grandfather and she must have stayed up most of the night and their faces showed it the next morning.

As Jason came into the kitchen that morning Grandmother was fixing scrabbled eggs and bacon. Jason reached around her waist and hugged her very tightly. She turned and looked at him with a sad smile. He asked her if she was okay?

"I'll be fine, and you?"

"Okay for now, I guess," was his reply.

"That's all we can pray for." Grandmother said. "We have to deal with this one minute, one hour, and one day at a time, but together we can do this. We have to carry on, for your parents."

Breakfast was eaten quietly. Grandfather didn't say more than a dozen words the entire time. Grandmother fought off tears the entire time, but struggled to put on a strong front, which Jason realized was for his benefit.

After breakfast, they gathered all the pictures that they had sorted out the night before, bundled up and drove downtown to the mortuary. Jason's other Grandparents were already there. He didn't know them very well, as they all but disowned his mother when she married his dad.

His maternal grandparents were of old money and held themselves far above the lot of common folk. They were upset to be sure, but Jason didn't feel they shared his sense of loss.

The mortuary staff was kind and very helpful. They walked everyone through the process. Things were going well until it was time to select the caskets. The two sets of grandparents differed widely on which caskets to choose. His mother's parents wanted only the finest and most expensive. Dad's parents wanted something far more modest, citing cost as the main reason.

Just as tensions seemed on the verge of getting out of control, when his mother's father ranted that if she had just once listened to him, none of this would be happening.

Jason took a deep breath and stepped between both sets of grandparents and announced that his parents enjoyed the simple things in life. What brought them joy was the things that God provided. Things like the sunshine, flowers, summer rain on the roof. Then he paused a moment and smiled. "And tacos, man did they love tacos."

That comment made both sets of Grandparents smile. Then Jason asked if he could have their blessing on picking the caskets that he felt mirrored his parent's passion. The Grandparents conceded and Jason picked out two matching pine caskets. Not the plain board style, but simple enough.

As they were about to leave the mortuary, his mother's parents asked Jason if he could excuse the adults for a few moments so they could discuss another important matter. He nodded and walked over to an empty waiting room.

He knew what they were going to discuss and could hear bits and pieces of that discussion through the walls. It was what was going to happen to him. He wasn't sure what each of them were thinking, and until that moment, he hadn't even thought of his future. He quickly thought of what might happen. He could only think of three outcomes. One he would stay where he was, with his paternal Grandparents. He knew them much better than his mother's parents, which he had only seen on rare occasions while growing up.

Two, he might have to go live with them or maybe one of his mother's siblings. Again, he didn't know those people, having rarely ever seen them.

The third option was becoming a ward of the State, and then who knew what would become of him. He thought it odd that the third option didn't seem all that much worse than the second.

He felt himself growing nervous and a bit frightened until he heard his Paternal Grandmother speak up. She let everyone know in no uncertain terms that Jason was family and was going to live with them.

That evening, as Grandmother was making supper, Jason came up behind her and wrapped his arms around her and kissed her cheek.

She instantly smiled. “Well, thank you. What was thank for?”

“For being you.” Jason replied. “You have no idea what being with you means to me right now.”

Grandmother stopped what she was doing and turned around and wrapped her arms around him. “I do know, honey. Because I need you as much as you need me.”

“Is Grandfather okay with me being here?” Jason asked.

“Well, of course he is.”

Jason just nodded his head.

“Your Grandfather doesn’t say much.” Grandmother admitted. “He is a very quiet man. Life hasn’t been very kind to him, but he is a good man. Give it time, he will come around and open up a little more in time.”

“What do you mean about life not being kind to him?”

Grandmother thought a moment. “Let’s talk about this at another time. It isn't something I can explain in a short time. Okay?"

"Okay."

After supper they worked on the obituaries, and as usual Grandfather said little. The following morning, they drove down to the local newspaper and placed the obituaries with them. Then it was out to the cemetery to pick out the lots. This was followed by a stop at a monument dealer to pick out the head stone and get it ordered.

Four days after the accident, the funeral was held. His mother's parents, an uncle and two aunts stayed pretty much to themselves. Jason sat with his paternal grandparents and that was all there was to the family side of the curtain. On the friends' side of the curtain it was almost standing room only. More than a dozen friends and neighbors got up and spoke about what kind and loving people his parents had been.

The hardest part of the ordeal was watching as they closed the lids on the caskets. It would be the last time he would ever see their faces and he couldn't stop himself from crying. Grandmother instantly wrapped her arm around him and pulled him close to her.

Then the trip out to the cemetery. A short graveside service and most of the people including his mother's parents left. Jason and his paternal grandparents stayed and watched as the caskets were lowered into the vaults.

Most of the people that had attended the funeral had gathered back at the mortuary for the big luncheon. Many people offered their condolences and prayers as they arrived, but as people started to get their food and eat, many just talked and laughed amongst themselves.

Grandmother mingled with the guests and thanked them for coming. Jason and Grandfather sat quietly off to the side by themselves. Nothing was said between them, then suddenly Grandfather patted Jason on the shoulder, as he took a deep, sad breath while nodding his head, which Jason took to mean that Grandfather understood what he was feeling.

The public address system in the airport announcing that his flight would begin boarding passengers brought Jason back to the present. As he waited in line, he thought a silent prayer that God would grant him some time to be with grandfather before the Lord called him home.

CHAPTER 2

Jason's seat was just a few rows behind the wings and a window seat. The sun had already set but the last of its blazing rays still lit the western sky. It took more than twenty minutes for the passengers to board, and another twenty before the plane moved onto the tarmac.

Soon the plane raced down the runway and lifted into the darkening night sky. Jason loved flying at night. The twinkle of lights was humanity's mark on the landscape. Some places had a myriad of lights, other areas the lights were quite sparse. As he stared out the window his mind drifted back to right after he had lost his parents.

Grandma Judy was such an enigma. On one hand she was tough and strong willed. On the other hand, she was gentle, loving, and gave him so much comfort at the worst time in his life.

The first week nothing much was done other than just get through each day as best they could. Grandma always tucked him into bed, but only after they prayed together at the side of his bed. Then they talked. Sometimes they talked for only a few moments, other nights the talk lasted for an hour. It all came down to him, how he was feeling, and what was going through his mind. Many nights they cried together and held each other.

The following week Jason started back to school. A few of his classmates offered condolences, but most went on as they had before, just ignored that he existed. He was never a popular member of the class and his recent experience made him even more quiet. All the teachers were kind and offered an ear if he needed it.

A couple of weeks after the funeral, Grandfather drove Grandma and Jason out to the cemetery and showed them the headstone that had just been erected. It was a nice stone and featured a lovely "Together forever" script caption at the center bottom of the stone.

That night after he and Grandma Judy had said their prayers and she had tucked him into bed, Jason looked at her with a sad expression.

"What are you thinking?" Grandma asked.

"That's all this is, isn't it?"

"All what is?"

Jason shrugged. "The stone with their names and dates. That's all there is now."

Tears instantly flowed from grandma's eyes and she nodded her head. She tried to dry the tears, but they continued to fall. "That is all there is for the world. For us, the people who loved them and were loved by them, they still exist in here." She patted her heart. "And in here." Patting her head. "They will be with us for all of the remaining days of our lives."

"Do you think they can see us? Hear us?"

Grandma thought on that for a moment. "I don't know, maybe. I do, however, think that once we cross over to God's home everything is different."

"In what way?" Jason was intrigued.

"In every way." Grandma replied. "Time is completely different there than here. A day in heaven might be a lifetime here. Maybe by the time they get settled in, we will be there with them."

"What do think Heaven will be like?"

"Beyond anything we can understand." Grandma smiled. "It will be beautiful beyond anything we have ever seen here. Love will be so much above our current ability to feel or understand. For the first time, our hearts and minds will be truly open."

The stewardess brought the drink tray and Jason was served a cup of Vernor's. The fact that the airline even offered it surprised him. It was Grandma Judy's favorite drink and a truly Michigan thing. He took a sip and mentally thought, "here's to you Grandma."

He glanced out the window into a night void of light with an occasional little dot emanating from someone's homestead. It made him think of life, his life. More to the point what his life was about to become.

When he was little, he was surrounded by family. Many points of light. When he was 12, two of the brightest lights went out. Then one by one, uncles, aunts, cousins, Grandparents, all either moved away and out of touch or passed away. One by one the lights of family faded. Now, he was flying back to his boyhood home to watch as the last of the lights slowly dimmed and went out.

Another sip of Grandmother's favorite Ginger Ale and Jason closed his eyes and could still see her standing at her stove in her old and faded apron. She loved to cook and bake and excelled at both. He felt a little guilty admitting it, but Grandmother could cook circles around anyone he knew, including his mother.

Sometimes Grandma would hum as she worked. It was always an old tune. Some of them he knew, like the hymns and some of the other old songs. She had varied tastes in music, loved gospel, R&B, even some of the old rock songs. Mostly she loved love songs. When Jason asked her about her passion for love songs, she just smiled. And then quoted Jesus, "The three greatest things in life are faith, hope, and love. Of these three the greatest is love."

Grandmother was always teaching him things as well, or at least trying to. She taught him the basics of cooking and baking, but he never really took to it. Mostly because he didn't feel the need. She was a fantastic cook, so why would he even want to replace her? She also taught him to sew, to do laundry, proper grooming habits, and how to shop.

He remembered one time when they were shopping for school clothes. He had wanted a fancy name brand. She asked him why?

"Because it is what all the kids are wearing." Was the reason he gave.

"Why do you suppose that is?" She asked patiently.

"Because that brand is popular."

"People imitate others because they want to fit in." She said. "They want to be part of the 'In' crowd. In doing so, they miss the point entirely. God didn't make us to be the same. He gave each of us a special life with special circumstances. Be it intelligence, money, or maybe charming good looks like he gave you."

Jason remembered blushing.

"The point is we must accept who, what, and where we are and make the best of each moment. If I was in your shoes, I would look at the things I need, and the amount of money I have to obtain them, which is often limited. Then look at everything available comparing appearance, quality and price. The smart way to shop is to find the best values so you can obtain more of what you need. It is always better to have two pairs of jeans so when one is dirty you have another, than to have to wear a pair of dirty designer jeans."

It was a lesson he never forgot, and not one person even noticed that he didn't wear those high-dollar brand names. The lesson was continued at the grocery store. Although where the stores private label of a favorite snack fell short, she just smiled and said some things are worth paying up for.

Jason looked back out the window, and in the distance could see the glow of a city. It made him think of Heaven. In the spring of his fifteenth year, Grandmother Judy started showing signs of having less energy. At first everyone just passed it off as age catching up to her. Then Grandfather started to worry when the symptoms continued into summer.

Finally, in mid-summer Grandfather insisted that they go see the family doctor. They didn't find anything at first and wanted to do more tests. Grandma wanted nothing to do with letting them poke and prod her. In late August Grandfather insisted again and the tests were carried out.

A week went by without a word from the Doctor's office. School had started back up so Jason wasn't home when they got the call. When he got home that afternoon, Grandmother was sitting on the sofa alone. Grandfather was in the garage working on an old motorcycle. She asked him to come in the living room and sit with her.

Jason suddenly knew that they had heard from the Doctor and it wasn't good. He just didn't realize how bad it was.

She explained that it was some sort of blood disorder that even the doctors didn't fully understand. It affected her bones as well. Particularly the bone marrow. Her blood cells and platelets were not being produced properly. It might clear up or go into remission or it might not. There wasn't much they could do for her and the risk of blood clots and strokes were greatly increased. For now, they had her on medicine to address that.

Jason remembered they talked and prayed together that afternoon, but as the days passed her condition didn't improve. On Halloween, even in her weakened state, she greeted the costumed children and handed out candy.

For thanksgiving, Grandpa was just going to bring precooked food home, but grandma insisted that she and Jason would make the feast. By now she was in a wheelchair and had to be strapped in to ensure that she wouldn't fall out.

Grandma made a list of everything they would need, and he and grandpa went and got everything on the list. What made that trip to the grocery store memorable was that grandpa was different than his usual self. He was talkative, engaged, and even showed a bit of humor. It was a pleasant surprise for Jason as Grandpa was always distant and quiet around him. He later discovered the reason things were different on that shopping trip was because grandpa was focused. He didn't have to come up with things to say or talk about.

The day before Thanksgiving, grandma sat in her chair and instructed Jason on everything he needed to do. Then early the next morning they were back in the kitchen cooking and baking. He did everything when and how she told him. It was the first time he truly appreciated everything that his own mother had gone through at every holiday to make the holiday meal the feasts that they were.

That meal was fantastic, and they repeated the process on Christmas eve, but by then Grandma was getting so weak and forgetful. The meal was still good, but not quite the meal Thanksgiving had been.

By the second week of January, grandmother could no longer even sit in her wheelchair. Jason would come home from school and sit and talk with her until she was just too tired to continue.

By the first week of February it was evident that the end was near. One afternoon Grandmother told him how much she loved him and how proud of him she was. Jason understood it was her way of saying good-bye. He started crying and told her that he wanted to go with her.

She got very serious and somehow, pulled herself almost to a sitting position. "Don't ever say that, please. God forbids it. It is even one of the ten commandments. Thou shall not kill. That includes yourself. Besides, I have had a wonderful long life. Topped off with having you here now. When I am called home, your Grandfather is going to need you. Promise me you will look after him."

Jason promised her that he would, although how he was going to keep that promise was beyond him.

Another week passed slowly with grandma having fewer and fewer moments of being alert enough to talk. Then one very cold and snowy morning Grandfather came into his room and awoke Jason to tell him that Grandmother Judy had passed.

Jason remembered the hopeless feeling that swept over him as he got out of his bed. Everyone he had held dear in his life was gone. He walked down the hall to his grandparent's bedroom and slowly made his way to the side of her bed.

He was surprised by how beautiful she looked. The past few months had been very hard on her, and how she looked to him had changed over that time. She had gone from his beautiful guardian angel, to a pain wrecked shell. Her complexion had changed as well. Over the past week Jason had noticed her skin color looked blue to him. Now, as he reached out and took her hand in his, she was once again beautiful.

The anguished look caused by the pain was gone. She truly looked not only like she was sleeping, but also at peace. Jason sat beside her, holding her hand until the mortuary arrived to take her away.

CHAPTER 3

The following day Jason and Grandfather went down to the mortuary and went through the same process they had done when his parents passed. The staff was beyond kind and helpful, but about half of the way through the planning Grandfather asked for a break so he and Jason could have a few moments alone.

As soon as the mortuary staff had exited the room, Grandfather turned to Jason. “None of this is right.”

“What do you mean?” Jason was at a loss.

“I don’t know.” Grandfather said as he got out of the chair and walked over to one of the tall windows in the room. Outside the window the snow was steadily falling. Grandfather stood silently for a few moments and then without turning around to face Jason he spoke softly. “I just had the strongest feeling sweep over me. I have never been one to buy into all that religion stuff your grandmother believed.”

"Okay." Jason said, not knowing what else he could say.

Grandfather turned around and looked at Jason. "When her death was imminent, she was in so much pain." Grandfather began. "I knew what was happening but helpless to stop it. Then a moment before she passed, I saw something I can't explain."

"What?"

Grandfather held his open hands out before himself conveying that whatever it was, it was beyond him. "It was like she suddenly had a slight glow about her. The expression of pain was replaced by a smile. That horrible color she had taken on over the last few weeks appeared to suddenly drain away. I went to the side of her bed and took her hand. Her eyes followed me until I sat next to her. Then she slowly exhaled and never inhaled after that."

"I noticed her color as well." Jason replied. "You think that it was Jesus who came to get her?"

Grandfather turned back to face the window. "Oh, I don't know about all of that, but something happened."

"So, what are you saying isn't right?"

"Burying her."

"But we have to."

Grandfather turned back around and look Jason straight in the eyes. "No, we don't."

"What do you mean?" Jason was starting to get concerned.

"Over the past few months, your grandmother and I talked a lot at night. She always read her Bible and prayed. Toward the end, I would sit with her as she did these things, so she naturally started reading and praying out loud. One of the passages says that dust we were and dust we shall become."

"Okay, I am familiar with that passage."

Grandfather took to his chair and turned it to face Jason. He leaned closer as he spoke. "What we are about to do is have that beautiful lady's body pumped full of chemicals to slow that process down as much as possible. It won't stop her from eventually becoming dust, just drag it out through a long process."

Jason didn't reply as he searched his grandfather's eyes for a clue of where he was going with this.

Grandfather paused a moment and looked down at the floor. When he raised his eyes there were tears in them.

"Over the past six months I watched the only person that ever truly understood me and loved me anyway; die a slow and agonizing death. In those final few moments, I saw that she was given a reprieve. I could see it in her eyes. All the pain faded away. She died anyway."

"I'm lost." Jason admitted.

"What I am proposing," Grandfather answered. "Instead of burying her and letting time slowly finish what disease had started, I am asking you to accept a request from me."

"What kind of request?"

"I would like to have Grandma Judy's body cremated," grandfather replied. "We will still buy a plot next to your parents and put up a stone. I don't want to inter her there just yet though. I propose that we keep her ashes with us. Close to us. Then when I pass, I ask that you have me cremated as well."

"Okay," Jason didn't know what else to stay. He did like the idea of keeping grandmother close.

"When I am cremated," Grandfather continued. "I want you to get a bigger urn and mix our ashes together and then inter us in the grave."

Jason was speechless but nodding his head. He loved the idea and for the first time in his life he had seen a glimpse of his grandfather that until then only Grandma Judy had seen.

The staff were very helpful in getting Grandpa's wishes taken care of. In fact, they offered a nice double urn so that when his time came, his ashes could simply be added.

The visitation and funeral were disappointing to both. Only a hand full of people showed up for either one. On the way home both were quiet and absorbed in their own thoughts.

The weather was dark and gray with snow falling all day and forecasted to continue through the night. "This weather is probably what kept people at home today." Jason finally said.

"Maybe," grandfather nodded. "I'd say it had more to do with how many people really knew her. She wasn't from around here."

"She lived here a long time." Jason countered.

'Yes, more than 40 years." Grandfather agreed. "However, she never worked outside of the house. The people at the stores are always changing, so one doesn't build much of a relationship. Considering how little she interacted with the community, I'd say she had a good turn-out."

"There were less than twenty people there."

Again, grandfather nodded. "It isn't about how many friends you have, but of what caliber."

The next few weeks went by slowly and painfully. Grandfather was content to work on an old motorcycle in the garage by day and watched television at night. He said very little outside of necessity. Once a week he went to the grocery store while Jason was at school. For meals they lived on simple basic things. Most of which could be heated in the microwave.

Jason was slowly coming to realize that he was reaching his limit on boredom and loneliness. By the end of March, the weather started showing signs of spring and Jason started hinting at different things they could do. Grandfather simply shrugged or didn't comment at all. At school Jason went through the motions, but his grades had slipped a bit and the guidance counselor asked to speak to him. Jason was afraid to say anything about what was going on at home for fear of the State taking him from there.

There were very few people that Jason had met that knew his grandfather. Of that small circle of acquaintances, the elderly neighbors were probably the closest. Jason found himself needing someone to talk to and not having anyone he felt he could.

The weather turned warm and sunny by the third week of April. Jason spent his weekend raking the old leaves and sticks out of the yard. When he noticed that the neighbor's yard was in the same condition, he just automatically raked theirs too. As soon as he had finished the job, the neighbor lady called out to him and asked him to come in and rest a bit.

As Jason made his way to their front door, she stepped out of the house and held the door for him to enter. Feeling a bit uncomfortable, he entered and stepped to the side and allowed her to take the lead. When they entered the kitchen, she motioned for Jason to take a seat at the counter/bar while she went to the refrigerator and got a pitcher of iced sweet tea.

She was a touch over 5-foot tall and of slender build. Her hair was snow white and her skin had a very light, almost translucent glow to it. Her most striking feature was her bright, penetrating ice-blue eyes.

She set the pitcher down on the counter and grabbed two tall glasses from the cupboard. "Thank you for cleaning our yard." She smiled as she poured out two glasses of tea and then took the stool across from Jason's.

"How are your grandparents?" She asked after taking a small sip of her tea.

"Grandma passed in February." Jason replied, realizing for the first time that the neighbors didn't know. The look on her face was complete sadness.

"I am so sorry," she said as she reached out and patted his hand. "I visited her for a little while before we left for Florida. I could see she was very sick. She was a saint."

"She was," was Jason's sad reply.

"How are you and your grandfather getting along without her?"

Jason looked into her eyes for a moment and she could see the sadness in them. He then just shrugged and looked down at the counter.

She gave him a few seconds, then gently reached over, and lifted his chin so she could look him in the eyes. "Tell me what you are feeling."

Jason shrugged again. "I'm not even sure that I know that."

"What do you mean?"

A tear formed in the corner of Jason's eye, and part of him felt like he was on the verge of losing it, while the other part of him felt that if he told her the truth, he would be betraying his grandfather.

"Honey, sometimes we all need someone we can talk to. What you say to me will stay between us if that is what you want." Her eyes were so sympathetic.

"To tell the truth," Jason began. "I feel like I don't really know him. He is a very quiet and reserved man. I believe he loves me, in his own way. Grandma said that he was deeply affected by what happened over in Vietnam, and maybe so. He has never talked about it around me."

She sat silently, just staring into Jason's eyes for a moment, and then reached out and took both of his hands in hers. "I know that feeling very well." She then looked out the backdoor window for a moment like she was thinking of what to say next, or if she should even say it.

"My husband and I were married before he left for Korea. He was the most wonderful man I could have ever dreamed of. His two years in Korea changed him. Then toward the end of his career in the Army, he was sent to Vietnam. He was wounded and spent a year in hospitals before being given an early retirement as a disabled veteran. The man I got back is not the man I married. He still has that good heart he always had, but his nightmares never leave his mind. Like your grandfather he has become quiet and withdrawn. So, I fully understand what it means to live with someone and feel lonely."

"So, what do you do? What can I do?" Jason asked.

"Love him on his terms." She smiled and patted his hands. "Your grandfather and my husband have both seen things that they should have never seen. Experienced things that no one should ever experience. We must allow for that and realize that they are coping the best way they can."

What neither the neighbor lady nor Jason knew was that her husband had started for the kitchen to get a beer. When he heard them talking, he pulled up short and stood around the corner and listened. What he was hearing broke his heart.

Before leaving Jason learned that her name was Isabel and that her husband's name was Hank. From that day on, Jason did their yardwork and then spent time visiting with Issy, as she liked to be called. Another thing that he didn't know then was that Hank took the talks Jason and Issy had to heart. For the first time he realized that what he had become deeply hurt his beloved Issy and he made himself a promise to work on changing that.

CHAPTER 4

A week after Jason had visited with Issy, Hank watched Jason go off to school. Then as soon as Issy left for the grocery store, he walked over to Denny's garage and found him busy working on an old motorcycle.

Denny looked up from his work as Hank made his way through the side door. Hank's right leg was problematic and prone to give out on him sometimes, so he always walked with a cane. Denny silently watched him as he closed the door behind himself and then turned and slowly made his way over to where Denny was working.

"Morning, Neighbor." Hank smiled as he found a dirty old stool to sit on close to where Denny was working.

"Morning, Hank." Denny nodded his greeting. "What's going on?"

"Oh, not much." Hank replied. "How about with you?"

"Not much." Denny replied, surprised by this visit. Hank had never been in the garage before, and after being neighbors for nearly forty years, this morning's exchange was the first words spoken between them without their wives' present.

"Cool old bike." Hank nodded at the machine that Denny had dissected into a million parts.

"You like bikes?" Denny seemed surprised.

"Loved them back when I could ride them." Hank confirmed. "That was before Nam of course."

"That what happened to your leg?"

"Yes, got hit twice in that same leg before I hit the ground."

"When was that?" Denny asked, suddenly interested.

"1965." Hank thought back to that day. "Would have bled to death if not for this crazy young black kid named Jenkins. He came running through that mass of bullets and dove to the ground next to me and bandaged my leg on the spot."

"Sergeant Stanley Jenkins?" Denny lit up with amazement.

"Gee, I don't know." Hank thought a minute. "Jenkins was a Corporal when I got hit. He told me it was his first week in the country. Don't honestly know or remember what his first name was."

"Short guy built like a tank. Always smiling and humming." Denny prodded.

"Yeah, had a scar on the right side of his chin." Hank remembered.

"Holy Cow!" Denny shook his head. "It was Stanley Jenkins."

"You knew him?"

"You are not going to believe this," Denny laughed. "I was also hit in 1965. Took three hits. One to the leg, one to the shoulder, and another to the right side of my chest. And guess who risked his life to first get to me, then drag me back into a small depression and patch me up long enough to be lifted out?"

"Stanley Jenkins."

"Yep, the same medic that saved you, saved me."

"That is unbelievable." Hank shook his head. "What are the odds of one man saving both of us?

"Long odds, that's for sure." Denny agreed. Then after a quiet moment he asked what brought Hank over?

"I need your help." Hank replied.

"Oh?"

"Your grandson has been helping us with the yard work."

"And?" Denny wondered where this was headed.

"Well," Hank hesitated as he thought though what he would say next. "When he is done, Issy has him in for refreshments."

"Okay."

"They talked," Hank frowned. "I heard part of it, and to be honest it broke my heart and opened my eyes a bit."

Denny wasn't sure he wanted to hear the rest of it, but knew he had to. "Go on."

Hank looked Denny square in the eyes. "You and me, are a lot alike. We've seen things and done things we can't talk about. It haunts us every day and invades our dreams at night. We have closed ourselves off to suffer in private. We were lucky that we had good women to help us along, but I've never really opened up to Issy about a lot of things. Oh, I told her the basics, but never really got to the point I could actually enjoy our life together."

Denny looked down at the floor and just nodded his head. Judy had been just like Issy, silently allowing him to keep it all inside.

"The other day I heard Issy talking to Jason." Hank went on. "I heard her tell him that she knew what it was like to live with someone and still be lonely."

Denny didn't look up. He simply nodded his head.

"I need your help," Hank urged. "I need someone that truly understands my position to help me open up and give the remaining years of Issy's and my life together meaning. To give Issy the love, companionship, and happiness that she has been missing all these years."

Denny looked up at Hank for a moment, then he slowly got to his feet and put the wrench he held in the toolbox. He paused a moment before turning to face Hank. "I'm not sure I would be of any help. It is too late for me to change for Judy."

Hank sadly nodded. "What about Jason?"

"What about him?"

"He has lost everyone he loved but you."

"I can't change that." Denny defended.

"No." Hank agreed. "We can't change our past either. Hopefully, together, we can find a way to change what time we have left to bring joy to those we love.

They deserve it, so we must try. I can't do it alone, but maybe together we can."

"How?"

"I don't know." Hank shrugged. "Maybe if we started small. Found things we like to do that could involve Issy and Jason."

"Like what?" Denny wasn't sold on any idea yet, but Hank could sense him warming to the possibility.

"What do you like to do besides the bikes?"

Denny thought a moment. "Haven't done anything for years, but I used to like to travel and fish."

"Really?" Hank smiled. "I enjoyed doing those two things as well. Also loved to go exploring and picnics too."

Denny smiled. "In many respects, the bikes have always been my way of exploring." Then he frowned. "Sadly, I did most of that alone without Judy with me."

Hank nodded his understanding. "Issy will be back before long, so I will get back home, but think about it, and next time I get a chance I will be back over. We can beat this thing, you and me."

Denny just nodded as Hank turned around and walked out. Once he had the garage to himself again, he went back to work on the bike. The rest of the day, until Jason got home, his mind never stopped thinking of what Hank had said. Things he knew in his heart to be painfully true. He had never been one to pray, but he thought of his dear wife and how she had endured his behavior in silence and loneliness. He looked up at the ceiling with a tear forming in his eye. “God, I don’t really know how to do this, but I need your help. I know Judy was a Godly woman, and that she is there with you now. I need your guidance right now. If you need any pointers, I am sure my dear Judy will gladly help you out.”

When Jason got home, he found his grandfather all washed up and dressed in decent street clothes. “What’s up?”

Denny shrugged. “Getting tired of our man cooking. Thought maybe we could go get some real food. Got much homework?”

“Actually, only a bit of reading, that I can do before class tomorrow.” Jason replied.

“Okay, then you want to go get some food.” Denny smiled.

Jason just smiled back. It was the first time he felt that his grandfather's smile was real and not forced. "Sure."

As they walked out to the car, Denny asked what kind of food Jason was hungry for. When Jason replied that it didn't really matter, Denny suggested a new steak buffet that had recently opened in town. That was fine with Jason.

The drive to the restaurant was a quiet one, both hoping the other would say something first. When they arrived, they simply got out of the car and walked into the place in silence. The meal didn't change things. Denny told the waitress what he wanted to drink, and Jason did the same. When told they could help themselves to the buffet, they both simply went up and got their food.

It was only when leaving the place that Denny asked Jason if he was full.

"More than full," Jason replied while rubbing his stomach. "The food was really good."

"It sure was." Denny agreed and then added. "We have to do this more often."

The trip home was once again a quiet affair. When they did get home, Denny went into the living room and turned on the television while Jason did his homework.

The following week went by with less than 100 words spoken between them. Friday was Jason's 16th birthday. It came and went without any acknowledgement.

Jason remembered looking forward to this day his entire life. When it came and went without the slightest acknowledgement, he felt lonely and forgotten.

On Saturday Jason mowed their yard and then also mowed the neighbor's. As he shut the mower off, Issy was at the front door asking him to come in.

Issy had just baked a batch of chocolate chip cookies and the house smelled heavenly. Jason and Issy spent half an hour talking and enjoying the fresh and still warm cookies. Just as Jason was about to leave, Hank came into the kitchen for a cold soda.

"Thanks for doing the yard." Hank forced a smile. He didn't know why, but he had to force it. He was glad the boy and Issy got along so well. In fact, he appreciated that more than getting the lawn mowed. In that moment Hank realized that he had a long way to go to become the man Issy so desperately wanted.

"You're welcome." Jason smiled with a nod.

"I'll gladly pay you for the service." Hank offered.

"No need for that." Jason smiled and rubbed his stomach. "Issy has already more than paid for it."

Hank nodded and then asked. "How is your grandfather doing?"

"All right I guess." Jason replied with a shrug.

Hank nodded, about the reply he expected. Denny had a long way to go as well. "School almost out?"

"A couple more weeks." Jason replied.

"What are you going to do with your summer?" Issy asked.

Jason just shrugged. "I don't know, probably not much."

That reply hit Hank hard. He silently made a promise to himself that this would be the summer of change.

The next day Hank took Issy out to eat at a nice restaurant. After they ordered their food Hank reached across the table and took both of Issy's hands in his.

With a very surprised look on her face Issy asked if he was feeling all right?

"No, not at all." Hank frowned. "I have had the best wife a man could ask for, and yet failed to enjoy this life I have been given." When Issy started to say it wasn't so, Hank asked her to hear him out.

"I want to apologize for not being the man I could have been. I allowed things beyond our control to change me. Instead of turning to the one person that has always been there for me, I shut you out."

Tears were forming in Issy's eyes as she smiled a sad smile. She felt his pain and knew what he was doing was very hard on him, but it was something she had prayed for years to have happen.

"I heard you and Jason talking the other day and it made me realize how much sadness and loneliness I have made you bear. I know this is not going to be easy or an overnight thing, but I promise you that things are going to start changing. I will need your help."

"I will help in any way I can." Issy smiled as a tear ran down her cheek.

Just as Issy spoke their food arrived and the waitress noticed the tears. "Are you okay ma'am?"

Issy smiled up at the young lady and wiped her tears. "I couldn't be happier. Thanks for asking."

When the waitress walked away, Hank smiled. "I know this isn't going to be easy, but I want to find something, a common ground if you will, that we can build on."

"What brought this on?" Issy asked.

"As I said, it started when I heard you and Jason talking the other day, and then again yesterday. I had already had a talk with Denny since we both have the same problem. When I asked Jason what his plans for summer were, and he didn't really have any and seemed to accept that there wasn't anything to look forward to, I knew that moment that the time had come for me to put the past behind me and make things change for the better."

"So, you want to include Jason?"

"I do, if that is okay with you?" Hank replied. "Not in every aspect, but I would like to find things to do that he might enjoy. You come first, but if we can find things to do that everyone enjoys, then I would like to include him as well."

"What about his grandfather?"

"I don't know if we can pull Denny out of his funk, but I would like to at least offer him a chance."

"What did you have in mind?" Issy asked.

"I'm not sure, to be honest." Hank shrugged. "I tried thinking of a few things that we loved to do when we were first married. Things like going on little adventures, fishing, and going for ice cream."

Issy smiled. "We haven't really done any of those things, other than going to Florida for the winters. I think I would still love doing those things today as much as I did back then. Remember how I would put together a picnic lunch for us when we went fishing?"

"I do indeed." Hank smiled. "I loved our little fishing expeditions. Walking along the riverbank until we found a nice romantic spot."

Issy winked with a smile. "Not sure we would be much good at walking along the riverbank today though."

“I thought of that too.” Hank admitted. “I do, however, think I have a solution to that problem.”

“Oh?”

“A pontoon boat,” Hank said. “That way we would have a stable platform to walk about on. Big enough to have our picnics on and room for guests. We could easily travel up and down the rivers in search of a good anchoring spot.”

“A pontoon boat is expensive and has to be put into the water and taken back out again. Are you up to doing that?” Issy asked.

“I have thought of that as well.” Hank laughed. “Our current car couldn’t handle it, so we would have to change that as well. Even if we didn’t get a boat, our current car is getting to the point of needing to be replaced, so I thought that maybe we could start shopping for the replacement with hauling a boat in mind.”

“You think you want a truck?”

“Not a truck really,” Hank confessed. “I was thinking more along the lines of a Chevrolet Suburban.”

“What is that?” Issy asked.

“Kind of a cross between a truck and a station wagon.”

"How is driving that different than driving a truck?" Issy asked.

"Well," Hank thought for a moment. "It has more creature comforts than a plain old truck."

"Will I be able to drive it?" Issy was concerned.

"Only one way to find out."

Being a Sunday afternoon with nothing to do, Jason went for a walk alone. Denny was where one could usually find him, in the shop working on an old motorcycle. As Jason walked along, he took in what other, normal folks were doing. Being a warm sunny day there were a lot of people out in their yards and often with family.

Some were mowing their yards, others washing their cars, or getting a start on their gardens. A few people cooking on their grills. Others just playing games in their yards with their children.

All of it made Jason sad and aware of what was missing in his life. He was happy for those lucky people, but deeply missed his own parents and grandmother. He thought back to happier times when his parents would take him places like the Zoo, or a park and play games with him. He also dearly missed his grandmother Judy. The times that they spent just talking. In the short time he had with her, his grandmother taught him so many things.

One of those things kept nagging him at the back of his mind. Grandmother Judy always said that everything happens for a purpose. The thing, whatever it may be happens for the long-term good. Even things that are very painful today will serve us well if we recognize that there is or was a purpose, even the loss of his parents. Grandmother Judy explained that we all have something we are to accomplish in our lives and when that is completed, we get to go home.

Sometimes that purpose is to be an example for others. Maybe to teach others to appreciate the things they have.

Try as he might, Jason could just not fathom a valid reason for his parents and grandmother to be taken from him. He found himself dearly wishing that his faith was as complete as Grandmother Judy's was.

Monday morning it was back to school. He packed his own lunch and grabbed his books. Grandfather Denny was already out in his shop and hammering on something. Issy had hit the nail on the head. Jason was living alone with someone else.

Denny never gave it a thought. He got up, made coffee, filled his big cup and went to work out in the attached shop. Today was going to be a big day. He had finally finished rebuilding the Knucklehead engine and by noon had it installed. When he was trying to kick it over the bike rolled slightly forward and tripped the kickstand. The bike instantly started to fall to the left, but Denny quickly pushed back with his left leg while throwing his body weight to the right.

When the bike's center of balance went from too far left to too far right, he put his right foot down to catch it. The problem being that a cardboard box of old parts was in the way and didn't give him something solid for his foot to land on. The bike went down with his right leg caught in an awkward position. Instantly both the tibia and fibula snapped, and the ankle fractured.

The pain was instantly intense, and he broke out in a sweat and his vision started to blur, and he realized that he was alone with no help within hailing distance. The only phone in the shop was on the far side wall and mounted 6 feet off the floor.

Denny came back to consciousness not knowing how long he had been out and if anything, the pain had increased. He desperately looked around himself trying to figure out how he was going to get out from under the bike first and get help second.

Try as he might, he simply couldn't get the bike lifted high enough to pull his broken leg out from under it. He had found several pieces of steel and wood close enough for him to be able to use them as pry bars, but nothing was long enough to be of any help. During one of the attempts, the bar slid out of where he had placed it and slammed into the damaged leg. The spike in pain brought the sweat and vision problems back in full force. He had to stay focused and keep himself from blacking out if he could.

Staying alert took all his energy and focus for the next several moments. When he finally had control of himself again, he started looking for an answer. The box of old parts that had caused his foot to land badly had torn open exposing some of the parts inside. Denny's eyes were quickly drawn to one part in particular, the horn. What he didn't know was whether the horn was any good. Maybe it would work, maybe it wouldn't. For the moment, it was all he had.

He fought back the pain and carefully stretched himself out far enough to reach the box. The problem was that the horn was trapped under other parts of various design and size. All these parts were held in place by the weight of the fallen bike. He had to pry it loose, so he pulled himself back to where he was and grabbed a couple of the blocks of wood and moved them closer to the box. Then he grabbed a couple of the pieces of steel to use as pry bars.

After pulling himself back into a position that he could try to free the horn, he had to stop a moment and catch his breath. The pain was killing him, but he had to keep trying. It took several tries, but he finally got the horn loose by rocking the various parts on top of the horn. One final rocking of the parts and the horn fell out onto the floor. He had a horn, now he needed a way to activate it.

Denny looked for a battery, any battery would do, but none were within reach. The closest was at least ten feet away. Then he carefully examined everything within reach or close that he might be able to use. He spotted the small battery charger about five feet away on the edge of the bench. The problem with that, it was five feet was beyond his reach to begin with and being on the four-foot tall bench made it even farther.

Denny felt he had to do something and do it quickly as the pain was starting to make him panic. Again, he started looking around himself for anything that could help him. There wasn't much but he did spot a dirty old roll of duct tape laying under the bench just beyond his reach.

He had to find something that he could use like a lasso to draw the tape closer. Looking around himself he spotted the old drive chain for the bike in the old parts box. He quickly grabbed one of the pieces of steel and started poking and prying the old parts box apart. In a couple of minutes, he was able to free the drive chain.

It took a dozen tries before he was able to get the chain to fall around the old roll of duct tape. Just being able to draw the tape within his reach was a small victory. Denny didn't waste a moment; he quickly taped the chain in the shape of a loop he prayed would be big enough to fit over the charger and taped the rest of it to the longest piece of steel he had.

His plan was to loop the charger and pull it closer to him without pulling it off the bench where it would fall to the ground. Again, it took several tries, but this time each try brought the charger closer to him. When he had it close enough that he thought he could catch it, Denny pulled the charger off the bench. The little charger was heavier than he had thought, probably because of his weakened state. All he was able to do was break its fall as it still ended up hitting the floor with a crash. Hopefully, the fall hadn't damaged this needed component of his only hope of getting help.

He quickly connected the charger to the horn. All he had to do now was find a way of supplying the charger with power. He had built this shop more than twenty years ago and spent every day in it, so he knew where he kept everything, and he knew that he kept a coiled electrical cord on a hook just to the left side of the bench. Try as he might, he just couldn't see over the bench and spot it.

Having to find a way to look over the bench, Denny went back to the now spilled box of old parts. He remembered removing and discarding the mirror that the bike came with. He now prayed that he had tossed it into this box. In less than a minute he found what he was looking for and worked to free it from the other parts.

It was cracked but the bent shaft that held it to the handlebar was almost perfect for the use Denny now had in mind. Holding the mirror up and slowly rotating it, he was able to spot the power cord. Getting it off the hook and close enough for him to reach it would be another matter. Luckily, if he could do that, he would be able to use it right away as he always left it plugged in. If he had needed to use a drill or another power tool, he could just grab the cord and plug the tool in. When finished with the task, he unplugged the tool and coiled the cord back on its hook.

Taping several of the pieces of steel together and using the edge of the bench as a fulcrum and the cracked mirror as a guide, Denny was able to lift the coil off the hook and allow the coils to simply slide down the steel to his waiting hands. What he had expected to be the toughest part of the task turned out to be the easiest. Without a second thought Denny plugged the charger into the cord and was instantly rewarded with a loud blaring horn.

Chapter 5

Issy was the first to notice the blaring horn but didn't pay much attention to it for several minutes. Hank noticed it as well but figured a horn had shorted out and Denny was probably trying to fix it. After five minutes went by both Hank and Issy became concerned.

"Something must be wrong." Issy told Hank. "Go over there and see what is going on."

When Hank got over to the side door of Denny's shop, he found the door locked. He peeked through the window and could see the fallen bike but not Denny. As soon as he knocked on the door, he noticed Denny's left arm reach out from under the bike and disconnect the horn.

"Help!" Denny screamed as loud as he could.

"The door is locked." Hank shouted back.

"Break it open." Denny yelled back.

It didn't take a great deal of force. Hank banged his shoulder into it and the door popped open. The moment he was inside the shop he rushed over to Denny.

"Phone on the far wall." Denny was exhausted and his voice was weak and raspy. "Call for an ambulance, please."

Once Hank had made the call he came over to Denny's side and helped get the bike off and Denny dragged out from under it. With each slightest move Denny cried out in pain.

When Hank didn't come right back, Issy knew something was terribly wrong and ran over to Denny's place. "What has happened?" Issy cried as she flew through the door.

"A bike fell over and broke his leg." Hank replied. "Help me get him more comfortable."

"No!" Issy said as she grabbed Hank's sleeve. "Don't move him. You don't know what all is wrong and you could make things worse." By then the sirens on the ambulance could be heard.

Issy ran out to direct them to the shop. The first two through the shop door were city police officers. Both men were also trained EMTs and were totally professional in getting the details and keeping Denny calm.

The ambulance crew were in the shop a couple of minutes later with a gurney in tow. The first thing that had to be done was to get the miscellaneous old parts, pieces of steel and wood out of the way so they could see what they had to deal with.

The first thing they did after getting the story on what happened was cut the leg off Denny's jeans. The skin was torn in several places, but the bone itself was not sticking out. After feeling the legs and finding where it hurt the most, they fitted an immobilizer cast on it.

Once they had Denny on the gurney, they carefully wheeled him out of the shop and around the house to the back of the ambulance. As they were loading him into the ambulance, Denny called out and asked Hank to secure the house for him.

"Don't worry about anything, Brother. We'll take care of it." Hank assured him.

Once the ambulance roared away, Hank turned to Issy. "When does Jason get home from school?"

"Not until 4 or so." Issy replied. "Think maybe we should go get him?"

"I'm thinking maybe we should. The boy is the only family Denny has."

“Well, you wouldn’t have known that from Denny. His only concern was about his precious shop.”

“Issy, don’t go there. Not now at least.” Hank frowned. The comment hurt more than she could know because he felt the same guilt. “He knows the boy is safe, once everyone leaves here, the shop is not.”

Issy didn’t reply, just gave him that look she was so good at to let him know she wasn’t sold on that explanation.

In order to secure the shop, Hank had to repair the door jam that he broke when he forced his way in. Once they had the house locked up, they went back home and cleaned up before going to Jason’s school.

Jason was in History class when the school principal came up to his desk and whispered for Jason to come to the office.

Jason became very worried and nervous during his walk to the office. Before he even got there, he could see Issy and Hank through the big glass windows. Grandfather and he weren’t close, but they were all each other had in the world.

The moment Jason stepped into the office Issy was at his side with her arms around him. She explained what had happened and offered to take Jason to the hospital. Jason just nodded his head. His mind was in a whirl, it was happening all over again. Was he a bad omen?

Just as his Grandmother Judy had done the night his parents had been killed, Issy sat next to him and holding his hand while trying to convince him that his grandfather would be okay.

When they arrived at the hospital, Denny was in a room in the ER. They had already done the x-rays and fitted a temporary cast. Denny was obviously in pain while trying to explain to a lady with a clip board that he didn't have his wallet with him since the accident happened in the shop. It took a while to convince her that he was who he said he was, and she finally let him off with a promise of a phone call when he got home and found his insurance card.

With a bit of uneasiness, Denny was transferred to a wheelchair and wheeled to the ER exit. They sat there while Hank went and brought his car around. Issy watched as Denny and Jason exchanged nervous glances. She fully realized that the road ahead for these two was not going to be an easy one.

Denny was put in the front seat next to Hank because of the extra room the front seat offered. Then Jason and Issy got into the back. They hadn't made it out of the hospital parking lot before Issy reached over and took Jason's hand in hers.

Jason had no idea what to expect next. It was obvious that his grandfather was in a lot of pain. The hospital had sent some pills along to help control that, and Issy had written down when each should be taken. The bottles that the pills came in had that information as well, so Jason wasn't sure why Issy had questioned the nurses about it like she had.

A hundred different things were going through Issy's mind on the ride home. She realized that Denny's condition was probably more than Jason could handle on his own. Also, he had school to attend during the day. She wasn't sure how Hank, or even Denny was going to react, but she knew she was going to have to take charge. There were also things that were going to be needed. Just what those things were would have to be determined once they got Denny home and situated.

Once they got Denny into the house and into his recliner, Issy took charge. She asked Jason for a piece of paper and a pen. She started off with the things that would have to be handled. Things like taking the pain pills and when. Having seen how unstable Denny was on the crutches, she asked if they still had the wheelchair that Judy had used. They did, and Jason went to the basement and brought it up. It was covered in dust, so Issy set Jason to work cleaning it.

Next came food, what did they have on hand that Jason could prepare? Along with that question came what kind of food did both Jason and Denny like? Next question was about convenience. They needed certain things to be close to Denny at all times. Fluids to drink and take his pills with, a urinal, a bell to ring when he needed help, and a dozen of other little things that could help make Denny's misery more tolerable.

When Issy had her list all made out, she made a shopping list for Hank and Jason and then sent them after the non-food items. She and Jason would do the food shopping when they got back. That would ensure that they got things both Denny and Jason liked, but also things Jason could prepare.

Once Hank and Jason had left, Issy turned her attention on Denny. "This is going to be a difficult time for both of you." She started off as she took a seat on the sofa.

Denny just nodded.

"I've gotten to know Jason a little this spring, and I know you and Hank share a common problem. The ability to open up to others. I knew Judy very well, and we shared notes many times. When Hank was in one of his moods, she offered a shoulder to cry on, as I did her. We chose to take you two on, Jason did not. That said, that boy is a part of you and a part of your late son."

Denny didn't respond for a moment as he digested what she had just said. "What do you want from me?"

"A little patience and understanding." Issy replied. "That boy is scared and nervous. He realizes that he must step to the plate and take care of you. You must understand that he won't know what you need without you asking for it. If you ask for something today, don't expect him to automatically know that you need it again tomorrow. It is going to take him a while to get the routine down."

Denny nodded his head. "Okay, anything else?"

"Yes," Issy smiled. "Be grateful. Tell him thank you. Let him know that you appreciate his help."

"I'll try." Denny promised.

The balance of the time they waited for Hank and Jason to get back, Issy rearranged things to make them easily accessible for Denny from his recliner. Then she got pillows and blankets out of the closets and bedrooms. She even went into the bathroom and moved a stack of toilet paper close to the stool so Denny would be able to reach it if needed.

When she had done all she could think of doing to prepare the house for the weeks ahead, she came back into the living room and sat down on the sofa. What is the longest you have ever sat in that chair?" She asked him.

"Three or four hours in the evening, why?"

"Does your butt get sore after sitting in it for that long?" Issy asked.

"It hasn't." Denny replied, suddenly realizing why she had asked. For the near future he was about to spend more time in this chair than all the time that he has had it combined.

"That could change. " Issy warned. "I will gather a few pillows to set next to your chair so they can be found if the need arises. Also, I am going to make up a bed on this sofa for Jason so he can be close enough to help when you need it most, which will probably be in the middle of the night."

Denny had dozed off by the time Hank and Jason came back. Hank stayed with Denny while Issy took Jason to the grocery store. While she had been waiting for the two to return, she had made out a shopping list after inventorying their cupboards.

On the way to the store Issy went over things that Jason could expect to have to deal with in the coming weeks, maybe months. One of the basic things was preparing food. When she asked what things Jason could already make, he admitted that he had never learned to cook anything. His mother had been a good cook, Grandmother Judy was an exceptional cook. Other than helping make their last holiday meals, Jason had never spent any time in the kitchen.

"Well, what have you been living on since Grandmother Judy passed?" Issy wanted to know.

"Cereal for breakfast," Jason replied. "Soup and sandwiches, frozen dinners and fast food. Grandmother Judy tried to teach me to cook, I just didn't pay close enough attention to learn."

Issy thought about that for a minute. "Okay, here is what we are going to do. We will get a few more of those things, but I assumed that was the case when I checked out your freezer. That kind of food is meant to get you by in a pinch, but not for a regular diet."

"Yeah, we knew as much." Jason agreed. "It was all we knew how to make."

"Tonight, I am going to start your lessons in cooking. And this time I want you to pay attention." Issy smiled. "How does porkchops, baked potatoes, and green beans sound for dinner?"

"Sounds great." Jason suddenly felt hungry and excited about a good home cooked meal.

When they left the supermarket, they had a full cart. Most of it was food, but Issy had also insisted on getting cleaning supplies. When she was putting those things in the cart, she had asked Jason when the toilet had been cleaned the last time?

"Grandmother Judy had done it," was the reply.

"Oh dear." Was all she said, realizing that she had a lot of teaching to do.

Denny was still asleep when they got back to the house. Hank was sitting on the sofa with his head back and asleep as well. It was too early to make supper, so after the groceries were put away, Issy went about teaching Jason how to clean the bathroom and kitchen. Because it hadn't been done in months, some of the stains were tough to clean.

"If you clean the bathroom once a week, and the kitchen daily, this job isn't so hard or time-consuming." Issy pointed out. She then showed Jason how to mop the kitchen floor. They were almost done with the task when Hank stepped into the kitchen.

"When it comes to cooking and cleaning," Hank said. "You have the best teacher there is." Which made Issy smile.

"Learn your lessons well and you'll make someone a good wife someday."

Hank added, which got him a stern glance from Issy, but made Jason laugh.

At 5pm, Issy said it was time to start dinner. She showed Jason how to apply butter to the skins of the potatoes and then wrap them in foil and put them in the oven. Since it would take the potatoes longer to bake than make the rest of the meal, she had Jason help set the table and a tray for Denny.

The meal was a pleasant affair, and the food was incredible. Jason gathered up the dishes and washed them without being asked to, which won praise in Issy's eyes. Before leaving for home, Issy helped Jason get Grandmother Judy's wheelchair out and made sure Jason and Denny were as prepared as they could be for the night. She also posted her phone number on the wall next to the phone in the kitchen.

"Call me at any time if you run into trouble." She told Jason.

"I will."

Denny and Jason watched television until the late news came on. No matter how he tried, Denny could not find a position that eased the pain. To make matters worse his bad right hip and bad back were competing with the broken leg to be the most bothersome. Twice he asked Jason to help by lifting his broken leg and changing the pillows under it. Both times Jason could feel the breaks in the leg pop, which caused Denny to cry out in pain.

Throughout the night, every time Denny tried shifting his weight the pain caused him to cry out. The worst was when he had tried to move the leg in his sleep. By morning neither one of them had had much sleep. Jason decided not to go to school that day as he felt his grandfather needed him more.

Issy called just after 8am to see how they were getting along. Jason explained that for the moment things were okay. They had issues when grandfather had to use the bathroom and it had been a tough night.

"Well, that is to be expected." Issy replied. "Believe it or not, you probably have just made it through the toughest night."

Five days after the accident, Denny had his first appointment with the Orthopedic Doctor. He was hoping for a cast but was told that the swelling was still too great for that to happen, maybe at the next appointment in a week. Again, Denny was instructed to keep the leg elevated and absolutely no weight on it.

Twice during that following week things became so tense between Denny and Jason that Issy was called over to smooth things out. Denny was wholly uncomfortable and both were exhausted. Issy decided that it was time for Jason to return to school during the day while either she or Hank could take care of Denny. With it being the final week of school for the year, Jason had to catch up, which meant spending most of the time taking tests that he hadn't prepared for. Luckily, the test scores were slightly down for him, but still above average and earned him a passing grade for the year.

At the next doctor's appointment Denny got his cast, which didn't eliminate the pain but did keep the broken bones from shifting around every time his foot was lifted. The only instructions from the doctor were to keep it elevated to keep the swelling in check, and absolutely no weight on that leg.

By then it had been two weeks since the accident. Denny and Jason still said very little to each other, but both had fallen into a some-what routine that accomplished the things that needed to be done. Jason had also gotten good at cooking and earned him the first compliment that his grandfather had ever given him.

The next three weeks went by slowly. The hardest part for Denny was having nothing to do. He had always kept himself busy out in his shop and now all he could do was bear the dull pain and watch really stupid television shows.

Both Denny and Jason were exhausted, nerves were getting on edge, and when Denny slipped getting into the bathroom, he cursed Jason's stupidity for not telling him that he had just mopped the floor. The fall had caused Denny great pain and Jason struggled to get his grandfather up off the floor. When everything seemed to fail and Denny's anger seemed out of control, Jason got up and walked away. Jason called Issy and while they were talking, Denny could be heard yelling in the background.

It was about 9pm, so both Issy and Hank were already in their night clothes.

They didn't bother to change and came right over. Denny was embarrassed, angry, and in a lot of pain. Issy and Hank got Denny back on his crutches before Issy left the bathroom to allow Hank to help Denny get on the stool.

Issy went out into the kitchen where Jason was sitting on the floor with his back propped up by the inside corner of the cabinets and his head in his hands supported by his knees. He was crying.

Even though Issy suffered from arthritis, she forced herself down to her knees on the hardwood floor in front of Jason and reached out and gently touched his arm.

Jason slowly looked up at her with tears running down both cheeks. "I tried. I really did. I just can't do anything right."

"Tell me what happened."

"I cleaned the bathroom like I do every Wednesday night. Which includes mopping the floor like you showed me how. It hasn't been a problem until tonight. Usually, he uses the bathroom in the morning. Tonight, he had to go in there and slipped on the wet floor."

"It wasn't your fault." Issy assured him. "It was an accident. Did you help him get to the bathroom?"

"No, he did it on his own."

"Has he been doing it that way?"

"Yeah, for the last couple of weeks he has been getting himself up out of the chair and with the crutches getting to the bathroom on his own."

"Did you know he was going there?"

"No, I had fallen asleep on the couch. I didn't wake up until he had fallen."

In the background they could hear Hank helping Denny back to his recliner. "Let's go have a talk." Issy said as she reached out for Jason's hand.

"He doesn't want to talk to me." Jason replied.

"Maybe not, but I do." Issy said as she reached out again, and this time Jason took her hand. And then had to help her up off the floor.

Issy didn't mince words. She told both that she expected better from them. She explained that what had happened; happened because of a lack of communication and scheduling.

Denny should not try to do something like he did without Jason being awake. Jason should do his mopping on a schedule, so it becomes routine. Also never mop a floor and leave it wet, especially if it is a floor Denny must walk on. Last but not least, they must be patient with each other. Both are having to deal with things they are not used to.

After Issy and Hank went home the balance of the night passed quietly. The next day Issy took Jason to the grocery store. This time they bought fewer frozen dinners and more variety of meats, vegetables, and a few desserts. Desserts were something Denny and Jason had not had since Grandmother Judy had passed.

They also got eggs, bacon, and a couple of bags of frozen potatoes already shredded into hash browns. Grandmother Judy had always made a hot breakfast and Jason was missing it and thought he could do it.

The following morning Denny awoke to a familiar smell coming from the kitchen. At first, he thought he was dreaming, but when Jason brought him a tray of eggs, bacon, hash browns with a side of toast and coffee he was amazed.

The food tasted like Judy had made it, and Denny realized that he had an opportunity to connect with his grandson.

"Man, it is amazing how well you have learned to cook in such a short time."

Denny said as Jason brought the coffee pot over to refill his cup.

"Really?" Jason was surprised by the compliment, especially coming from his grandfather.

"Absolutely. Your grandmother would be so proud of you."

That made Jason smile. "Thanks."

"Ever tried working on mechanical stuff?" Denny asked without thinking.

"No," Jason answered. "It would be fun to try. I probably wouldn't be the best student at first."

"Why do you say that?" Denny was a bit worried that Jason might mean that he didn't really want to learn from him.

"Because I have never done it and don't know one wrench from another."

Denny thought a moment. "Part of the problem we have, is that we don't have something in common to talk about. If you're game, I'll teach you all I know."

Jason nodded his approval.

Then for the first time in his life, Jason heard his grandfather make a joke. "Then we can find something else to do this afternoon."

CHAPTER 6

Once Jason had the dishes done and the kitchen cleaned, he helped his grandfather into the wheelchair. Then the two of them made their way down the hall and out into the attached shop.

"Okay," Denny smiled. "Let's begin by organizing this place first. I will need to be able to wheel around out here so I can teach you. So, the first order of business is to move the two finished bikes over in front of the roll-up door."

"Okay," Jason nervously replied. He wasn't sure how he was going to do that.

Denny saw the caution in his grandson's face and just smiled. "Like I said, we are going to take this slow. One step at a time until you are comfortable doing that. So, the first thing I want you to do is just sit on the one closest to us.

Jason complied.

"Now, you are going to stand the bike up. Put your feet down on the floor on both sides of the bike and grab the handlebars. Remember, the easiest way to handle or move a bike is to use its weight and center of balance to your advantage."

"Okay." Jason did as instructed.

"Now, bring the bike up to full upright position. You will notice that the weight issue goes away once you have it centered."

Denny had Jason practice doing that until Jason could bring the bike up, kick the stand back and move the bike with confidence. Once both bikes had been moved to where Denny wanted them, he had Jason get the bike that had fallen on him back up on its kickstand. Then it was on to picking up the old parts and the torn box that had once held them. Finally, Denny had Jason clear off the work bench and put the tools away. With each tool Jason picked up, Denny would explain what it was and where in the big toolbox it went.

Then Denny had Jason open one of the toolbox drawers, starting at the top, and take out any tool Jason didn't recognize. There were many tools Jason removed and asked about. In all it took over an hour to make it all the way through the toolbox.

Then just as Jason was closing the last drawer, Denny asked him for a 9/16" box-end wrench. Jason went directly to the correct drawer and produced it. The quiz went on until Jason could produce any tool Denny asked for.

The next step was to teach Jason about the bigger tools hanging on the pegboard behind the workbench. These included gear-pullers, slide-hammers and such. Then came the test equipment like spark testers, ohm and volt gauges, and the test lights.

Denny was really enjoying teaching his grandson about tools. It was the most the two had talked in Jason's lifetime. Jason was enjoying it as well and was surprised at what a good teacher his grandfather was. With each tool, Denny had explained what the tool was, how it was used, and with the test equipment, he had Jason actually do tests on the bike he had been building.

At noon they took a break for lunch. Jason made soup and sandwiches and while Denny was using the bathroom, Jason took the food out to the shop and set up a stand for his grandfather.

When Denny came out of the bathroom and saw where Jason had set the food up, he was both proud and had to laugh. “You know playing out here is very addictive.”

Every day for that entire week was spent out in the shop. At first Jason was so intent on learning that he hadn’t noticed that a miracle had taken place. While they ate breakfast, they discussed what they hoped to accomplish that day. In the shop they discussed what they were doing and debated different ways of doing it.

At lunch they talked about what they had accomplished and the steps that lay ahead of them. All the talking during the day helped them talk about other things at night as well.

On Saturday, they had the build bike to the point that it was time to fire the engine. Both were a bit nervous as it had been doing that very thing that had led to Denny’s accident. Denny was extra careful in explaining how to go about kick-starting a bike.

The first two kicks didn’t produce any results and Jason felt disappointed until his grandfather explained that it might take a few kicks to get fuel into the carburetor. On the third kick the engine roared to life so suddenly that it kind of scared Jason. In seconds the shop had filled with exhaust smoke and Denny motioned for Jason to kill the engine by swiping his hand across his throat.

As soon as the motor died, Denny wheeled himself over to the passage door and swung it open while pointing to the big roll-up door and motioning for Jason to open that up as well.

Once the smoke had cleared out, Denny had Jason get a fine headed flat screwdriver out of the toolbox. He then showed Jason the jet adjustment screws on the carburetor and explained how to adjust them. He explained what hand signals he would use to help Jason dial it in.

Jason then fired the engine on the second kick and went about doing the adjustments while listening to the engine and watching his grandfather's hand signals.

While they were so focused on adjusting the carburetor, neither of them had noticed Issy and Hank coming into the garage accompanied by a young lady about Jason's age.

It wasn't until Jason shut the bike off that they noticed the visitors. Hank was smiling and winked at Denny. Issy asked if they thought being out here was a good idea? Although inwardly she felt that anything that brought them together had a lot of merit. Then they introduced their granddaughter Isabella, or Bell for short.

Bell had a plain but pretty face. She shared her grandmother's fair skin as well as her name. The first two things Jason noticed though were her bright red, curly hair, and piercing ice blue eyes.

"So, you are teaching him to be a motorcycle mechanic?" Hank asked.

"I am," Denny smiled. "He learned to cook so quickly, and I will attest to his being good at it. I figured I would build on that and widen his range of skills."

"Well," Issy laughed. "You two got it running and no one got hurt doing it."

"He'll be as good of a mechanic as he is a cook." Denny proudly predicted.

"I am sure he will, he is a very gifted young man." Issy smiled and winked at Jason. "The reason we came over was first to introduce Bell, and to see if you gentlemen would enjoy joining us for a cookout later."

Jason and Denny looked at each other and nodded. "We sure would." Jason replied for them both.

"Well, I do the grilling." Hank said. "If you would like to learn how to grill, Jason. Give me a hand doing it. Say about 5 o'clock."

"I'd like that." Jason smiled. "We'll be there."

As soon as the neighbors left, Jason turned to Denny and asked what he thought would be a good side dish to take over with them?

"Well partner," Denny tried to imitate John Wayne and failed miserably. "You're the food expert here. What are you thinking?"

"Not sure as it is almost 3 now, that leaves us just two hours to make something."

"Even less time than that." Denny said. "I really need to get cleaned up and a fresh set of clothes."

"Okay," Jason tried to think of a solution quickly. "I have an abundance of eggs. I found Grandmother Judy's old cookbook and came across her recipe for her Deviled Eggs, I always loved them."

"You and me both." Denny agreed. "But can we get all that we have to do done in time?"

Jason thought a moment, then came up with a workable plan. "Let me get you a pan with warm soapy water, and another with warm rinse water. I can set it up right here on the lunch bench we set up. While you are doing the most cleaning that you can by yourself, I will get the eggs boiling."

Denny smiled, "you are good at last minute plans."

That made Jason smile. He couldn't help but appreciate how much their relationship had changed in the last 24 hours.

"There is one small problem with that plan."

"What is that?" Jason asked.

Denny motioned to the side door behind him. "The window. I'd rather bathe in private."

Jason laughed out loud and walked over to the stack of old newspapers that Denny kept as masking for painting. With a roll of masking tape, the window was sealed off in minutes.

"Like I said, you're good on your feet." Denny laughed.

Jason got the pans of water to the bench so Denny could wash as much of himself as he could. He also brought a razor and shave cream. Then he put a dozen eggs in a large saucepan and added water and placed it on the stove.

While that was happening, he went into Denny's room and searched for something that would fit over the cast. He settled on a large pair of bib overalls. A nice shirt, shorts and socks. One of the socks he cut in half so just the toes would be covered.

By the time the eggs were boiling, Denny was about ready to move into the house and out to the kitchen. Jason shut the stove off and checked the time. He had fifteen minutes to get Grandfather to the sink and wash his hair. That all hinged on Grandfather's ability to stand on one foot long enough.

Ten minutes into the fifteen, they had the hair washed and Denny's dirty clothes off.

"Now comes the embarrassing part." Denny quipped as he would have to have Jason wash his private parts.

"Less embarrassing than having you stink at the neighbors BBQ."

Denny laughed so hard that he almost lost his grip on the edge of the sink. "Don't make me laugh."

Jason went right to work washing his grandfather as best he could. Knowing that the clock was ticking on two fronts. The eggs and Grandfather's ability to continue standing on one leg. As soon as he had him washed and dried off, the clock on the eggs was up. Jason threw the damp towel onto the seat of the wheelchair and helped Denny sit down. He then quickly poured the hot water out of the pan and replaced it with cold water, to which he also added a tray of ice cubes.

While the eggs were chilling, Jason got the clothes he had chosen and laid them out on the kitchen counter.

"Bibs?" Denny asked.

"They're perfect." Denny replied. "The legs in them are big enough I think to fit right over your cast. They should be fairly easy to get on."

Beats what I got on." Denny shrugged. "Let's get them on."

Jason was able to get Denny washed and dressed and his deviled eggs made in enough time to arrive at Issy and Hanks's just before 5.

CHAPTER SEVEN

Hank was every bit as good at grilling steaks as he had claimed to be. Jason stayed by his side and learned a few little tricks that produced tender and tasty meat. Issy had wrapped buttered potatoes in foil and placed them on the grille as well. Bell had helped her grandmother with preparing the vegetables and baked rolls to go with it all.

It was a delightful meal that earned everyone praise for their efforts. Issy told Jason that maybe he could teach her how to make those deviled eggs.

While the adults enjoyed refreshments and talked, Jason busied himself with cleaning Hank's grill. He was so intent on doing a good job that he didn't notice Bell come over and pull up a chair close to the grill.

"Your deviled eggs were really good." She told him.

Jason turned around as he hadn't seen her come up. "Thank you."

"Grandpa said you didn't have to clean the grill. He planned on doing it tomorrow." Bell said.

"I know, but it gives me something to do." Jason replied. "Besides, it didn't take long and now it's done."

"You're kind of a jack of all trades." Bell laughed.

Jason pulled up a chair facing hers. "Hardly, just have a lot of really good teachers helping me out right now."

"You going to be a motorcycle mechanic when you get out of school?"

"I have no idea what I am going to do." Jason admitted. "It is too far down the road right now. I am just focused on doing what I need to do now and hope that tomorrow is better than today."

"Have a bad day?" Bell asked.

"Oh no! On the contrary. This week has been the best I have had since I lost my grandmother. And a lot of the credit for that goes to your grandmother."

"Really?" Bell smiled.

"Do you believe that everything happens for a reason?" Jason asked.

"My grandmother sure does. Personally, I'm not so sure, why?"

"Before my grandfather broke his leg, we were living together alone." Jason replied. "That was a term your grandmother used. Then suddenly he needed me to step up, but I was totally unprepared to do so. Your grandmother stepped in and taught me the basics of cooking and cleaning. Then when I mastered that, she taught me more.

We have been living on cold cereal for breakfast for months now. Thanks to your grandmother, I was able to make a good hot breakfast. It impressed my grandfather so much he got the idea of teaching me to work on motorcycles. Something he loves doing. That opened the door to communication. So, if my grandfather hadn't broken his leg, your grandparents wouldn't have stepped in and taught me how to care for him. Which in turn opened the door for us to be able to communicate."

"That all happened just this week?" Bell asked.

"It did." Jason smiled. "That is why I say it has been the best week I have had in a very long time."

Bell smiled. "My grandmother said that you have had a very rough go of it."

"Yeah," Jason nodded. "I haven't figured out why all of that had to happen, but bad as it was, Grandmother

Judy assured me that it's all in God's plan."

"You're a Christian then?"

"I honestly don't know." Jason shrugged. "My parents were, Grandmother Judy was very much so. Are you?"

"Absolutely." Bell replied with conviction.

"How can you be so sure?"

"Because I feel it deep within me." Bell answered. "I have had so many prayers answered. Things that couldn't have just happened if God wasn't listening to my prayers."

"Like what?"

"Oh, so many things." Bell's eyes opened wide. "When I was about seven or eight, my family took a week's vacation to the U.P., just off the shore of Lake Superior. It was early summer and so many plants were blooming, bees were pollinating, buzzing from one plant to another, and the area was heavily wooded.

I don't know what I was thinking but I followed the flight of a butterfly into those woods. Before I realized it, I was lost."

"Really? Didn't your parents see you wonder off?"

"They were busy fishing," Bell explained. "I had been sitting there watching them. I guess I got bored with that and wandered off."

"Wow."

"Yeah," Bell giggled. "Suddenly I heard noises like a big animal in the woods behind me. I froze in place and listened carefully. I could easily hear the animal moving about and was afraid of it being something like a bear."

"Up there it sure could be. Was it?" Jason asked.

"I looked around me and tried to find the way I had come and couldn't find it. I was so afraid that I started to cry. Started praying for Jesus to help me. The closer the animal sounds came to me, the harder I prayed. Then I spotted a red Fox sitting on its hind quarters watching me. Every now and then the fox would quickly look in the direction of the growing louder animal sounds. Then suddenly the fox started to run away. It stopped and turned to look at me. It must have stared at me for a full ten seconds before it turned again and ran less than ten feet and stopped again. It turned around and stared at me with what appeared to me to be pleading eyes, so without thinking I ran to follow it. It was much quicker than I was, so every now and then it would stop and turn to see if I was coming. As soon as we cleared the woods, I could see my parents fishing less than a hundred yards away. The fox stopped at the edge of the woods and looked at me. I thanked him as he turned and ran down the beach."

"That's quite a story." Jason said.

"You don't believe it?"

"It isn't that I don't believe it, it is a fantastic story." Jason replied. "It is just that I haven't experienced anything close to that."

"That was my eye opener for sure." Bell laughed. "Most answered prayers are not so dramatic. Simple everyday things that we worry over, fear or feel we need. Sometimes, the best answered prayers are the times we didn't voice it to Jesus, but he heard our heart and provided what we needed when we needed it."

"Or didn't give us what we wanted simple because it wasn't the best for us in the long run." Jason added.

"You do believe!" Bell laughed.

"That wasn't my words, but the words of my late dear grandmother. She always said that everything that happens does so for a reason. Sometimes the event is painful, but necessary for our future."

Bell smiled, "I think she was right."

Jason nodded and looked at the ground between them for a moment, before looking back up at her. "You don't get to visit your grandparents very much, do you?"

"I used to." Bell replied. "When I was younger, I did all the time. I guess I just got busy with friends and school. I talk to them on the phone sometimes."

Jason just nodded.

"Grandma always asks me to visit when we talk, so I decided this summer I would spend some time with them." Bell explained.

"I was the same way." Jason admitted. "I always had something more important to do. It wasn't until I had to come and live here that I realized what I had missed."

"What was that?"

"Until my parents died, I didn't really know my grandparents very well. Oh, we would gather at the holidays and such. But I usually did my own thing while the adults visited. I never got close to them. The three and a half years that I lived with my Grandmother Judy, I found that I dearly loved her and everything about her."

"You really miss her, don't you?"

"I do miss her so much." Jason admitted.

"When you think of her now, how do you see her?" Bell asked.

Jason thought for a moment. "You are going to think it odd."

"I promise I will try not to."

"I see her much younger than she was when she passed. She seems happy and smiling, almost radiant." Jason replied.

"I believe that to be true." Bell smiled.

"The thing I remember most about what Grandmother Judy told me she thought of Heaven, was that no one on earth understands Heaven." Jason said. "Not in any real sense anyway. She said that we lack the ability to understand the power of pure love. That the love we will feel in Heaven is far greater than we are capable of knowing here.

She also felt that in Heaven we will be on God's time, not just the rotation of this tiny planet around our sun. One day in Heaven could be a lifetime on earth."

"Oh wow!" Bell was impressed. "I love that description. I would have loved getting to know your grandmother."

"She was an awesome woman." Jason agreed.

"So how are you and your grandfather doing without her." Bell asked.

Jason laughed. "It's day by day, but if you had asked me that a week ago the answer would have been different than today."

"Oh?"

Jason nodded his head. "Today was the best day we have had since Grandmother Judy passed. I think most of the credit for that goes to your Grandmother Issy."

"How so?"

"She taught me how to cook." Jason laughed. "One morning I was so tired of cold cereal for breakfast, that I made us a hot breakfast of eggs, hash browns, bacon and toast."

"Wow! You're going to make someone a great wife someday!" Bell laughed. When Jason gave her his best stern look and told her that that was what her grandfather had said too, she laughed even more, which drew the attention of the adults.

“Well, the kids seem to be getting along.” Issy commented.

“They sure seem to be.” Denny agreed.

“I’m glad to see that.” Hank added. “I was also happy to see the two of you working together in the shop.”

Denny just nodded his head.

“Can’t work together unless you communicate.” Issy noted. “What made that happen today?”

Denny thought his answer over, then turned and looked directly into Issy’s eyes. “You.”

“Me?”

“Yes you.” Denny smiled. “And I owe you a great debt for helping us so much. I had my usual rough night of trying to find a comfortable position to sleep in, only to have my old body begin hurting in a new spot bad enough that I had to find another position. Needless to say, I usually am more tired in the morning than I was the night before.

Jason is usually up before I am and has already eaten before getting me our usual cold cereal and coffee. I guess he was tired of that menu and decided to make a hot breakfast. Something he was only able to do because you taught him how."

"Aw, well you're welcome." Issy smiled a humble smile.

"Anyway, I awoke Monday morning to the rich smells of eggs, potatoes and bacon." Denny explained. "For an instant I felt like losing Judy had just been a bad dream and that she was making me my favorite breakfast. It took a few seconds before I realized that I wasn't dreaming, and that Jason was cooking. Judy always hummed as she cooked. It made me truly realize the truth to what you both had told me before. That boy has a part of my beloved Judy and our son in him."

Neither Hank nor Issy responded to that other than with knowing smiles.

"It also dawned on me that the boy is a quick study." Denny went on. "He can learn anything and do so quickly. The breakfast was done to perfection and tasted as good as if Judy had made it. It just dawned on me that if you could teach him to cook that quickly, maybe I could teach him things I know, which would give us something to talk about.

I don't know anything about what kids these days are interested in, nor do I know anything about cooking. If I could teach him about bikes and mechanics, then we would find a level that we would have something to talk about."

"Does he like working on bikes?" Hank asked.

"He seems to so far." Denny replied. "He also is every bit the quick study with mechanics as he was with cooking. When we went out into the shop that morning, he didn't know one wrench from another. By the end of the day, he not only knew most of the wrenches, but a lot of the other tools as well."

"What do you do with all the bikes that you build?" Hank asked.

"Sell them." Denny answered. "A decent way to supplement my pension and keep me out of Ju...." He stopped short of finishing the statement, but both Issy and Hank knew what he meant.

"Ever put a sidecar on one of them?" Hank asked, which drew a questioning glance from Issy.

"A couple of times." Denny replied. The last two sidecars I installed were ones that I had made myself. The old ones are getting hard to find and expensive."

"So, how long are you staying?" Jason asked Bell.

"Just until tomorrow night." She answered. My parents will pick me up around supper time."

"I see." Jason felt like he would enjoy having his new friend around more but didn't expect it. "Have plans for the summer?"

"Yes, I do indeed." Bell smiled. "I am going on a mission for 6 weeks to Peru."

"Mission?"

"Yes, a Christian mission to spread the word and help those in need." Bell replied.

"Sounds exciting." Jason said. "More exciting than my plans for the summer."

"Maybe more exciting," Bell understood his feelings right away. "But every bit as important. Your grandfather truly needs you now. Also, I think it just might be God's way of bringing the two of you together."

"I hope you're right."

CHAPTER EIGHT

Not wanting to lose what they had gained the week before; Jason again made a hot breakfast for them. While they ate, they talked about the motorcycle project in the shop. Denny brought up the idea of building a side car for it.

"That would be cool." Jason agreed. "Can we do that?"

"We can if we plan it all out ahead of time." Denny replied. "I will need your help getting all the dimensions just right. Then I will show you how to design it."

After breakfast was finished, Jason did the dishes while Denny did his best to freshen up in the bathroom. He was still trying to balance on one foot and shave at the same time when Jason came to the door with his work all done.

"You know, before we get into the sidecar, maybe we should work on a better way for you to do what you're doing." Jason suggested.

Denny thought about it, and then nodded his approval. "What do you have in mind?"

"I'm not sure, but I was thinking maybe a unit with a stand and stool and maybe even trays for water, so you could sit comfortably and shave or wash up more easily."

"Well, I like the idea, but I am sure I don't have the supplies we will need to do that." Denny said.

"Okay," Jason thought for a moment. "What if we design it, figure out what materials we will need, and then ask Hank if he will take me to get those supplies?"

"Okay, let's do it."

Jason helped Denny get out to the shop and seated at the stand he made for him to eat his lunch on. After getting him situated, Jason asked. "What about the stand you are at now? What do you like about it, and what would you change?"

"For one, the wheelchair." Denny quickly replied. "If I sit in this for very long my bottom starts hurting."

"Okay, what if we got a nice office desk chair. One that can be raised and lowered, one that can swivel and maybe even rock?"

"Sounds expensive."

"Might be." Jason admitted. "But if we do it right, you will probably be using it long after the leg is healed."

Denny was amazed how his grandson's mind worked. Given the chance this boy was amazing. "Okay, but on this floor that chair may not roll very well."

"I wasn't thinking of having the chair roll independently. I was thinking of building it right into the stand itself. Then for the bad leg, we could build a footrest that extended out the back side with a padded cradle for you to rest that leg on. Remember the doctor said that you had to keep it elevated."

"Wow, you have thought of this."

Jason laughed. "Not really, kind of making it up as I go. But it is somewhat simple in that we know what you will need, we just have to fill those needs in a workable way."

"And for the top?"

"The top is dictated by needs. I figure it will be two tops, hinged together. The top surface will be flat so you can draw on it, or whatever. Then when you need to use it to wash and shave, the top lid raises up like a backsplash. The bottom surface will have three holes cut into it.

The outer side holes the size we need for plastic pans to hold warm water. The center cut to the exact size of the mirror we will mount into the backside of the top lid. So, when it is set up as a personal hygiene table, you will have the mirror to shave by. We could have drawers to hold your personal stuff and add a couple of bendable desk lamps for lighting."

"I am impressed Jason!" Denny truly meant that. "It sounds like you could just go ahead and build it without me interfering."

Jason blushed a bit. He wasn't used to his grandfather talking to him, let alone complimenting him. "Actually, I need you to help me plan it out. I can see it in my mind's eye but have no clue how to design something like this."

Denny smiled. "Then let's get to work. In the far-right hand drawer under the work bench are all my drawing supplies. You'll find paper, rulers, pencils and drafting stencils."

Jason stepped to the drawer and pulled almost everything out of it and laid it all down on the temporary bench.

"How about we design the tops first." Denny said. "Please get the plastic pans you think will work for wash basins."

When Jason got back with the pans, Denny had already made a lot of progress on the design. He quickly measured the pans and drew in their relative size into the bottom top panel. Within half an hour they had the drawing completed and the parts list made up. Denny had included Jason and his ideas in every step of the design and explained how he was drawing it so when it came to building it, it would be like reading a blueprint.

As luck would have it, Hank, Issy, and Bell had just been talking about finding something to do together for the morning, and when Jason called asking for help, they thought that doing that sounded like fun. Hank, Bell, and Jason would go for supplies, while Issy would stay with Denny just in case.

The desk chair was their priority. Hank was only slightly taller and heavier than Denny, it was decided that he should be the one to find the most comfortable. Denny had suggested a budget for Jason to work with and that chair would have taken more than half of it. So, before buying the new chair, Bell suggested that they go try a rehab store and see if they could find one there.

It took two stops, but they did find one that was nearly as comfortable as the new one, and a fraction of the price. They also found an old mirror of a size they thought they could use, and three of the flexible desk lights. Next, they went to the local scrap yard and after sifting through a huge pile of bits and pieces of square tubing, found enough pieces with the right length to build the frame.

The Hardware store came next with adhesive, bolts, piano hinge, lid support brackets and screws. The lumber yard was the last stop and the plywood had to be cut in half to get it into the car.

What had been a project planned for Jason and Denny to do, turned into a project that Denny and Hank coached while Jason and Bell cut and fitted the pieces. When welding the pieces together was required, Denny showed Jason how to do it. The first dozen welds took a lot of grinding and rewelding to make them look good, which kept everyone laughing. Well, maybe except Jason, but by the time the frame was completed, he had gotten the hang of basic welding. He had learned how to adjust the heat and wire speed to the point of consistent welds.

With the frame complete, Jason cut the two plywood panels down to 2 foot by 3-foot panels. Then he cut out the opening for the plastic wash pans. When it came to cutting the hole for the mirror, he hesitated.

"What's wrong?" Denny asked.

"I'm not sure I understand how you want this done. If I cut the hole wrong, I'll mess the whole thing up."

"Okay." Denny smiled. "First, let me say that you did exactly the right thing. When in doubt, stop. Think things over and/or ask questions like you just did. You have no idea how many parts, and how much steel I have had to throw away over the years because I plowed ahead without a full understanding of what I was doing."

Hank was smiling and winked at both Jason and Bell.

"We want the mirror on the backsplash, but we also want the top panel to lay flush on the bottom panel when being used as a desk. So how do you think you would go about it?"

Jason thought for a moment. "Place the mirror on the backsplash, and then carefully measure it from all points and draw in those lines on the bottom panel and cut the opening out."

Denny was nodding his head in agreement. "It can be done that way, but there is an easier way."

"How is that?" Jason asked.

"Place the mirror on the bottom panel. Make sure it is square and where you want it. Then trace around it with your pencil. Once you have that, remove the mirror and then add a half inch around those lines and make a second set of lines. Then use the circular saw to cut openings in all four of the outer lines. Finish the cuts with the skill saw. We want to keep the piece you are cutting out re-useable."

"Okay. "Jason said as he placed the mirror on the bottom panel. Using a square, he made sure it was straight. Following grandfather's advice, he then traced it and then added the second set of lines half an inch bigger all the way around. After cutting the piece out of the bottom panel, he turned to his grandfather. "Now what?"

Denny laughed. "What would you do next?"

"Install the mirror."

"Not quite." Denny replied. "First, let's join the two panels with the piano hinge. The best place to do that will be on the floor where you can lay them out flat."

Jason and Bell each took a panel and laid them out on the floor as Denny had suggested. The hinge was installed, and the lid supports mounted to the side of the panels so when the top lid was open it could be easily locked into place.

Then Denny had the kids set the panels on the frame upside down so the holes in the bottom panel were facing up. "Now, mark each corner of the mirror hole with your pencil. A small dot will do."

Jason did as instructed.

"Now open the two panels and use the square to draw light lines."

Jason carefully drew the lines with the square.

"Now, take the mirror and place it directly in the center of those lines. Be sure to measure each side from the mirror to those lines."

Jason and Bell worked to get the mirror in perfect alignment. As soon as they accomplished that, Denny had them trace the mirror.

"Now drill six holes in the frame of the mirror stay close to the edge of the frame so you don't hit the glass itself. Two holes per side and one each at top and bottom."

The top was finally finished and attached to the base with screws. The chair was mounted on a square tube that came out from the table on the floor and the pedestal of the chair that would normally be mounted into the castored base was simply welded onto the square tube. As a final touch, Denny had the kids take the piece they had cut out for the mirror and make a skirt around all four edges. Using an old but clean work shirt for the skirt material. This was attached to the bottom of the panel using staples. Now he had a basket of sorts to keep his grooming supplies in.

With the help of Hank and Jason, Denny transferred from the wheelchair to the workstation.

"This is great! You had a fantastic idea here. I love it!"

"It's not done, is it?" Bell asked.

"Yes, it is." Denny replied.

"Well, we do have to attach the lights yet, but for the most part, yeah, it's done." Jason said.

"The way it is?" Bell couldn't believe it. "You're not going to put a nice finish on it?"

"Not necessary," Denny laughed. This is a man's workstation. Beauty isn't the priority."

"All that work, and you are going to leave it looking like it was made from scraps?" Bell teased them. "Trust me, you men could use a little beauty around here."

"That's what we got you for." Jason said without thinking first and instantly regretted it.

Bell just looked at him with wide-open surprised eyes while Denny and Hank roared with laughter.

"I'm sorry Bell," Jason had turned beet red. "I didn't mean anything bad by that, I swear."

Bell smiled and gave him a wink. "Okay then, I'll let you off the hook this time."

When the men stopped laughing, they asked her what she was recommending. She said that leaving it with plain wood and the pencil marks made it ugly. They could sand out the pencil marks and put some kind of finish on it.

Hank and Denny looked at each other and nodded. "Okay," Hank said. "You two have done enough. Let us old guys finish it up. I have some hand-rub Tung oil finish at home."

"Yes, you two have done enough. Take a break and let us old guys finish it. I'll sand it while you're going after the finish." Denny told Hank.

"Well, if you think you two can handle it." Bell teased. "I will be back to inspect the job, so it better be up to my standards."

Jason got some sandpaper out for his grandfather before he and Bell walked out of the shop. "I am really sorry about what I said."

"You're forgiven." Bell laughed. "At least I have forgiven you, maybe it is time for you to forgive yourself."

"Maybe, I just don't know what possessed me." Jason said as he led her to a couple of lawn chairs set up under a beautiful maple tree.

"May I ask how old you are?" Bell asked.

"16 and you?"

"14, but I'll be 15 in a couple of months." Bell answered.

"Do you live in the area?" Jason asked.

"Not really. We live about 30 miles west of here. And you?"

Jason gave her a strange look, which made her laugh out loud.

"So, you're going home today?"

"In a few hours," Bell replied. "My parents are picking me up this afternoon."

"Which parent belongs to Issy and Hank?"

"Neither one actually." Bell answered with a straight face. "Both are kind of independent now, but my mother did when she was much younger."

Jason just gave her a stern look, which made her laugh.

They sat in silence for a minute before Bell asked about how Jason saw his future?

"I don't really know." Jason honestly replied. "I want to go to college, but for what I don't know. I can tell you though, I don't want to be a nurse."

Bell laughed. "Getting your fill of that?"

"And then some."

"I want to be a nurse." Bell said. "That or a Missionary, maybe both."

“Oh man, I did it again, didn’t I?”

“No.” Bell laughed. “I like you. You make me laugh.”

Jason just looked at her for a moment. He felt good that she liked him. It was the first time a girl had ever said she liked him.

“Okay, so no nursing, anything else you like to do?”

“Not really.” Jason admitted. “Haven’t really done much to figure that out. But I will tell you that I really enjoyed what we did today. It was cool planning it out and building the workstation for grandfather. I did enjoy that.”

“I enjoyed it as well.” Bell admitted. “It was something different, but not sure I would want to do it for a career. But I would imagine that there could be a lot of demand for such talent.”

Issy was busy in the kitchen making dinner for when Bell’s parents got there, when she noticed the kids sitting under the tree talking and laughing. “Well now, wouldn’t that be something.” She thought.

Just as Bell’s parents pulled into the driveway, Hank pushed Denny out of the shop and into the sunshine. Bell and Jason walked over to her parents' car as they were getting out of it. Issy had heard them pull in and she too came out of the house.

Jason couldn't help but notice how pretty Bell's mother was. First Bell hugged her father and then her mother. Issy had made it to the car and also hugged her daughter. The three of them standing together amazed Jason. It was like a photograph taken of the same girl through the stages of life. Bell's mother looked exactly as he suspected Bell would at her age, and Issy looked exactly as he envisioned Bell's mother would look in a couple of decades. All three versions were simply beautiful.

After the introductions were made, Issy invited Denny and Jason to join them for supper.

"Thank you," Denny replied. "But you all need some family time. Jason and I can manage just fine tonight. Spend this time as family. But thanks for the offer."

"Did you and grandpa make the workstation beautiful?" Bell asked.

"We did indeed." Hank answered. "Want to see it?"

"Well yeah," Bell quipped. "I have to see if what you think is beautiful meets my standards." Making everyone laugh.

Jason took hold of the back of Denny's wheelchair and wheeled him towards the shop as Bell's parents and grandparents followed along behind.

The workstation looked completely different. It had a rich glow to it now, and the lights had been attached so they could swing out of the way when folding and unfolding the tops.

Bell walked around the stand for a minute before proclaiming that the old guys had done a very good job of it. Bell's parents were equally impressed, not just with the finish, but the entire stand itself.

That night during their supper Denny commented on what a nice young lady Bell was. Jason didn't say anything but did nod his agreement.

"Pretty to boot." Denny added.

Again, Jason just nodded.

"You two seem to hit it off just great." Denny was trying to read his grandson's thoughts.

"Okay, grandpa." Jason gave Denny a stern look, but with a hint of a smile.

"Bell is very pretty, smart, capable, and fun to be with. Okay?"

Denny smiled, "Okay. Hank told me she is 14, so I guess it is a bit early to pair up 14 and 15-year olds."

"I'm 16." Jason said.

Denny stopped eating and just stared at his grandson. "When?"

"A couple of weeks ago."

"Jason, I am so sorry. I was simply not aware of it. No excuses. I promise to do better.

CHAPTER NINE

The next morning after breakfast, while Jason did the dishes, Denny wheeled himself out to the shop to where the wall phone was. It was a bit of a reach to get the receiver lifted off, even more so to dial the number of an old friend.

They had only been in the shop about an hour when a man knocked on the shop's side passage door. Jason answered the door and when the man asked for Denny, Jason led him into the shop.

"Jim," Denny said as he reached out and took the man's hand.

"What happened to you?" Jim asked.

"Long story made short; I broke my leg." Denny replied. "Did you bring it?"

"I did."

"Well bring it on in." Denny was smiling.

The man went back outside and in moments was wheeling a new Honda 250 motorcycle into the shop.

"What is this?" Jason was surprised.

“Happy Birthday Jason.” Denny replied.

“I don’t even know how to ride a motorcycle.” Denny was amazed.

“You will.” Denny said as the man handed him a slip of paper. Denny reached into his pocket and pulled out his checkbook and wrote the man a check for the bike.

As soon as the man had left, Denny had Jason get him and the bike out to the back yard. The rest of the day was spent with Jason learning to ride the motorcycle. By the end of the day, he had gotten good enough to feel very comfortable on it.

Over supper they talked about what they needed to do to get Jason’s driver’s license and motorcycle endorsement. Since he had already had driver’s training in school and obtained his learner’s permit, Denny decided that the next day would be spent driving around town in the car.

By the end of the week, Jason was confident enough with his driving skills that they went down to the DMV and he took the written and driving tests. It was official, he became a licensed driver that day. By the end of the next week, Jason took and passed the motorcycle tests and got his motorcycle endorsement as well.

The following week it was back to work in the shop. Denny sent Jason with the car for supplies while he drew out the plans for the sidecar they were going to make.

By the time Jason got back, Denny had finished the drawings except for certain measurements that they would need. He coached Jason in how to get them and had him measure each item twice to confirm the measurement was accurate.

Then Denny had Jason lay out the steel tubing that they would use for the frame that attached to the bike frame. Each piece was cut to the specs Denny had figured out. As Jason was cutting the steel, Denny explained how and why the frame was designed the way it was.

The design would make the sidecar a solid part of the bike's frame when attached but could also be removed so the bike could be ridden without it.

The second day was building the tapered framework that would have the sheet metal attached. The coils of metal were 24 inches wide and thin enough to be very flexible. Before the metal could be attached to the frame, Denny explained that they would first have to make paper templates out of the poster-board he had Jason pick up.

Jason had never done anything like making templates and found it exciting and frustrating at the same time. The reason for the process, Denny explained, was to cut out pieces of flat sheet steel that would wrap around the bullet styled nose of the sidecar and not wrinkle.

The process of making the templates took the rest of the day and both were tired from the effort, so Denny suggested ordering a pizza. When the pizza and soda came, Denny ate at his new workstation and Jason pulled up a stool and used it as well.

The following morning after breakfast they made their way out into the shop.

"You ready for the big sheet metal day?" Denny asked.

"Nervous is more like it." Jason replied.

"Don't be." Denny said. "What's the worst thing that could happen?"

Jason looked right at his grandfather. "I break my leg." Which made Denny laugh out loud.

"Okay, okay. What's the second worst thing that could happen?"

"I screw it up."

"Then we'll just go get another roll of metal. You've got this, I promise."

To transfer the paper patterns to the metal, Jason rolled the metal out and placed weights on the edges to hold it in place while he traced the paper pattern onto the metal. Then Denny had Jason cut between the patterns to make handling them easier. Each paper pattern had what it was written on it, and that information was transferred to the metal as it was cut out.

One piece at a time was attached to the tubular frame with the use of clamps. Once Jason was sure it was where it belonged, it was riveted to the tubing. It amazed him how well the metal pieces fit to the frame. The hardest part of it all was drilling the dozens of small holes for the rivets.

Jason was installing the final piece of sheet metal when Hank strolled into the shop.

"Wow! That looks fantastic!"

"Thanks." Denny and Jason replied in unison.

"It is almost done." Hank was amazed.

"Well, more than half of the way there." Denny corrected. "We still have the windshield, the seat, the headrest, and the canvass cover to go. I have a friend that will make the cover once we have the windshield ready."

"How are we going to make the windshield?" Jason hadn't thought of that.

"Old school technology." Denny laughed. "See that old stove over against the far wall?"

"Yeah."

"Open it up and remove the bronze block from inside."

Jason went over and did as he was told. The bronze block was shaped like he expected a windshield would look.

"Okay try the light to be sure it works. There is a switch for that on the backsplash." Denny said.

Jason turned the light on, and it was working.

"Okay, close the door and turn the oven on to a setting that I marked as P-1"

"What does P-1 stand for?" Hank asked.

"Just the setting I found that works best for this type of plexiglass."

"You form the windshield yourself?" Hank was amazed.

"Something I learned how to do when I was about Jason's age." Denny remembered back to that first job so many years ago.

While the oven was heating up, Denny had Jason get the square piece of plexiglass that he had picked up on the supply run yesterday. Then he had him get an extra-large cookie sheet that he kept under the work bench.

The cookie sheet was then cleaned with a wire wheel on an angle grinder and a palm sander. Finally, the cookie sheet was cleaned off using brake cleaner and wiped dry. Denny then showed Jason and Hank how to set the mold and plexiglass sheet on the cookie sheet.

"Be careful sitting this in the oven." Denny told Jason. "If it slips a little you can quickly adjust that, but you must do it right away or it will be too late."

"Okay." Jason seemed a bit nervous.

"Don't worry, you will have at least 20 to 30 seconds before the plexiglass starts to become really pliable."

"Okay."

"Once in the oven watch it closely, you want it to slowly droop down and conform to the mold's shape. As soon as that is accomplished you need to remove it, so have the oven mitten ready. You will find them on a magnetic hook on the side of the oven."

"OOkay." Jason was nervous.

"Hank, why don't you help the boy out and watch the process with him."

"I don't know as much as he does about it." Hank confessed.

"Don't worry, one of you might notice something the other doesn't. It isn't as precise as it may sound. A few seconds one way or the other won't hurt it. Just make sure that it has formed to the cast block and get it out before it begins to distort."

While Jason carried the cookie sheet over to the oven being careful to keep everything in place, Hank went ahead and was ready to open the door as soon as Jason got there.

The forming process took less time than either Jason or Hank had imagined that it would. As they removed the cookie sheet from the oven, Denny had them sit it on the work bench. After a couple of minutes Denny had Jason remove the plexiglass and hang it from the corners.

Denny looked the formed plexiglass over and said it looked great and should work out just fine. "With that gentleman," Denny said. "Our day is done. We'll let that glass cool tonight. Tomorrow, we trim it and drill the holes for the screws and canvass snaps."

That evening Hank took Issy out to eat, but before they got to the restaurant, he stopped by the local Chevrolet dealer and showed a couple of Suburbans to Issy. One of them was loaded with everything and was painted a nice blue with a white band across the middle of the chassis.

Intrigued with the truck, Issy asked to drive it, which the salesman was thrilled to have happen. It was much bigger than anything Issy had ever driven, so the first place she went was to the grocery store and tried to park it in the lot. It wasn't easy, but she accomplished that feat. Next, she went downtown and after half a dozen tries got the monster parallel parked. Finally, the road test. On the highway it was the nicest vehicle she had ever driven.

It would take the dealer a couple of days to get the trailer hitch and electrical plugs Hank wanted installed, but they made the deal that night.

Over dinner, Issy asked Hank if maybe they had gotten the cart before the horse?

"Why do you say that?"

"We haven't even looked at boats yet, and here we are buying a vehicle to tow it with." Issy said.

"Maybe," Hank conceded. "We did need a new car anyway."

Issy nodded her agreement.

"This Suburban will also be much easier to pack for our trips to and from Florida."

"Very true." Issy agreed. "Making those trips much nicer. It does drive nicely and rides like a car."

"True." Hank agreed. "So, all we did was replace a car that needed to be replaced and did so with keeping our other options open."

"Okay, but it is almost June." Issy stated. "We better be looking at some boats soon or this summer will be gone."

The following morning after breakfast Denny and Jason were back at work on the sidecar. Denny trimmed off the excess Plexiglas while Jason watched. Once trimmed, Jason laid the formed glass against the cowl of the sidecar, and it was a near-perfect fit.

With his grandfather coaching him, Jason attached the glass with screws and clips that would hold the heavy vinyl cover. Then Jason selected some scrap steel pieces that they could make the seat and headrest frames out of. While Denny was drawing out what he wanted the frames to be, a piece of scrap steel fell from the pile and hit the floor with a loud bang. Denny jumped nearly out of his seat, while ducking his head. The pencil he had been working with snapped under the pressure and tore the drafting paper.

It took him a second to recover and Jason noticed beads of sweat on his brow.

"You, okay?" Jason asked.

Denny tried to shake it off and act normal. "Yeah, sure."

"Want to talk about it?"

Denny thought for a second. "No."

Jason finally had a glimpse into what his grandmother and told him about.

"Let me get another sheet of paper and a pencil."

Denny just nodded his head as he wiped the sweat off his face.

Around noon the upholstery man showed up and made a pattern of the canopy cover and took the seat and headrest with him.

The next step in the process would be painting, so the main pieces of the bike and sidecar were removed.

"Okay," Denny said. "Time for us to go pick out the paint and have some lunch. I'm buying and you're driving."

Jason didn't have much trouble getting Denny into the car, but it did take him a few minutes to figure out how to fold the wheelchair up and load it into the back of the car.

"Lunch first?" Denny asked.

"Sounds good to me." Jason agreed. "I'm really hungry."

They decided on a locally owned mom and pop restaurant that was known for good food at fair prices. Denny decided that he would try and get into the place on his crutches. The biggest problem was the step up from the parking lot surface to the sidewalk. Once inside, he was able to get situated on a chair fairly easy.

After the waitress took their order and delivered their drinks Denny looked Jason in the eyes. "I'm sorry I reacted like I did to the fallen piece of steel. I didn't mean to scare you."

"You didn't scare me, as much as it worried me." Jason explained. "Grandmother Judy had tried to explain such things to me, but I didn't understand until this morning. She called it something like a flash-back."

"Yeah," Denny frowned. "I left that hellhole a long time ago and it still haunts me."

"Is there anything I can do?"

"No, there really isn't. I can't explain it myself. Loud bangs are the worst. Even over there any loud bang had us diving for cover. Rarely was it anything more than what happened this morning. Other times it was catastrophic."

"Like what?"

"A hundred different things." Denny shrugged. "A mortar, a shell, or some stepped on a mine. Maybe just a rifle shot, but it usually was the start of something really bad where someone was killed or badly injured."

"Is it just loud bangs?" Jason asked.

"No, but they are the most common triggers. Sometimes it is things as normal as crickets at dusk, the noise certain birds make. The worst, however, is dead silence. When we were on patrol and the jungle got dead silent, we knew something bad was about to happen. The jungle was never silent unless a lot of people were moving through it."

"That explains why you always have a fan going, even in the winter."

"Yeah," Denny frowned. "Your grandmother always allowed that even when it made her cold."

"She was truly one-of-a-kind." Jason said.

"She was indeed." Denny agreed. "The heart of a saint."

Jason just nodded his agreement.

"I miss her dearly." Denny frowned. "But I will tell you this. When your father was growing up, I could see so much of his mother in him. He not only looked a lot like her but had so many of her mannerisms."

"Yeah, I can see that now."

"The funny thing is, the more I get to know you, the more I see them in you as well." Denny smiled.

"Really?"

"Really." Denny laughed before adding. "You are like an old flathead motor."

"Oh, this should be interesting. How so?" Jason asked.

"Your heritage is deep, and time tested." Denny explained. "And like that old engine, when modernized with just the right improvements it becomes better than ever."

"I hardly buy that." Jason laughed.

"No, it's true." Denny argued. "Maybe it was due to qualities that your mother had when blended with your father's genes that make you what you are, I don't know. I will tell you this, you have their kind heart, their disposition, and their gentle way. To that you have things they didn't have."

"Such as?"

"You're smart, far smarter than I or they ever were. You have a gift of being able to learn and learn quickly. Just in the past few weeks I have seen you, as if for the first time. And I apologize for that."

"You don't have to apologize." Jason replied.

"Oh, but I do." Denny countered. "I can't explain what has happened.

Something about you changed who and what I have always been. A self-absorbed jerk."

"Grandpa, you're being a little hard on yourself."

"No, it's true. Like I said, I can't explain it. Something about you has opened my eyes for the first time. You've helped me see the impact I have on people, both good and bad. You've made it easier for me to open up, to communicate, to feel, as no one else could."

Jason didn't know what to say.

"Do you believe in Angels?" Denny asked quietly.

"Grandma Judy?"

"Maybe." Denny smiled a sad smile. "The day before she passed, I sat on the edge of her bed, and we talked. It was the longest and sweetest and most painful talk we had ever had. She said that she didn't know if she would be able to watch over us, but she would if she could. She also said that we needed each other more than we realized.

She also said that if she couldn't watch over us herself, she would ask Jesus to send an angel to do it for her."

"Do you believe she did that?"

"I don't know," Denny confessed. "I will tell you this. The morning you first made us a hot breakfast I was dreaming of her. Maybe it was the smell of your cooking that did that, but I was certain that she was with us, and her passing had just been a bad dream.

When I awoke and realized that she wasn't the one doing the cooking, I saw her in you for the very first time."

"Well, maybe she was with us." Jason replied. "She had told me basically the same thing during our last talk. So maybe she is watching over us. I do know that I often feel her presence."

Denny smiled at that. "Me too."

CHAPTER TEN

When they had finished eating it was off to the body shop supply store. The salesperson gave them several paint sample books to look through.

"What kind of paint are you looking for?" Jason asked.

"I don't really know." Denny replied leafing through the pages and checking out all the different colors. "I am hoping that something jumps out at us. Maybe, we will know it when we see it."

When Jason turned the very next page a color stood out. "Whoa! Look at this one." He said, as he handed the book over to Denny.

Denny took the book and looked at the colors on the page. "You are talking about the Deep Garnet Metallic?"

"That's the one that caught my eye." Jason nodded.

"That is cool." Denny agreed. "And look at the two right next to that one, they are just slightly lighter shades of that."

Jason looked at the colors grandfather was pointing out. “Okay, are you thinking of two-toning it?”

“Not exactly.” Denny had a devilish grin on his face.

“What?” Jason noticed the look his grandfather was giving him.

“Ghost flames.”

“Ghost flames? How are you going to be able to do that? We’ll be lucky if you can even do regular painting.”

“Who said I was going to do the painting?” Denny laughed.

“Well, I sure can’t.”

“You haven’t tried yet.”

While the paint was being mixed up, Denny and Jason stocked up on all the other supplies they would need. Including a fresh set of hooded coveralls, two respirators and special masking material and a new buffing pad.

By the end of the day, they had all the pieces to be painted in primer. Jason got grandfather set up to clean himself up on his workstation, before going out to the kitchen and starting on supper.

He was right in the midst of making bacon cheeseburgers when he heard a loud crash and moaning coming from the shop. He quickly shut the stove down and ran out into the shop. Denny was laying half the way between the wheelchair and the seat of the workstation.

"What happened" Jason asked as he carefully helped Denny into his wheelchair.

"I thought I could transfer myself from one to the other." Denny winced. "Would have if the wheelchair had been a bit closer."

"I'm sorry. I didn't think about that."

"Not your fault." Denny replied. "I am the dummy that didn't judge the distance correctly."

"You okay."

"Oh yeah, just a bit bruised.

That night after grandfather had fallen asleep, Jason went out into the shop and closed the door leading back into the house. The following morning when he wheeled grandfather back into the shop, he had a surprise for him.

"What have we here?" Denny said as he noticed what hadn't been there the day before.

"A steel arm that is adjustable in height and can pivot. The chain and steel triangle can also be adjusted for height.

You can swing it out of your way while you work, and then swing it back in and support yourself while you go from workstation to wheelchair."

"When did you do this?"

"Last night after you fell asleep." Jason admitted.

"Son, you are an amazing young man!"

The day was spent sanding the primer and shooting the deep garnet base and clear. When they had done all they could, Jason wheeled grandfather out to the back yard under a maple tree and then brought a chair and cold sodas out.

Hank and Issy got a call from the car dealer that their Suburban was ready for pickup. From there they went and visited several boat dealers. The plan was to simply shop and compare prices, but when one caught their eyes, they bought it and a trailer to haul it.

Once the boat dealer had it hooked to the back of the Suburban, he gave Hank a quick lesson in driving with the boat attached. Hank got the driving part down okay but backing it up was a problem and took him forever to get it where he was told to park it.

The same was true when they got it home. Denny and Jason were surprised to see them pull up in a new suburban, let alone having a new boat as well.

After watching Hank make half a dozen tries at backing the boat into his driveway, Jason pushed Denny across the lawns to see if they could help. When Hank had reached his frustration limit, he allowed Jason to get behind the wheel and try.

Jason had noticed that the biggest problem Hank was having was he kept over-steering it. On the second attempt, Jason got the boat parked in the right spot. They could easily drive past the boat and park the Suburban in their garage.

"Money burning a hole in your pocket?" Denny asked Hank.

"Not really, in fact probably more than we should have spent. The car we needed to replace anyway but could have done that a little cheaper than buying what we did." Hank replied.

"A lot cheaper." Denny laughed. "What about the boat?"

"Remember our first talk, about things we used to like to do?"

"Yes, I do." Denny replied.

"Well, we both loved to fish, and so does Issy. We can't get around like we used to, you especially right now. This type of boat offers the best of the options for us. We can fish like we used to. We can even have a picnic aboard as well. Care to join us this weekend?"

Denny looked over at Jason and saw him smiling. "You bet!"

"Good." Issy laughed. "Because we will need Jason to back it in the river for us."

The next morning after breakfast, Denny had Jason wet sand all the painted parts and then showed Jason how to mask off for painting flames. By noon the ghost flames had been painted. They took a long lunch allowing the base paint to fully dry. The masking was removed, and Jason applied the final four coats of clear.

While the fans were clearing the shop of fumes, Jason wheeled Denny out of the shop, and they stripped off their painting gear.

Once they were able to go back in and inspect the result, both were thrilled with how well the flames turned out. For lunch they headed back down to their favorite restaurant, and then to the sporting goods store to gear up for fishing and get their license.

The paint was allowed to dry overnight. The following morning Jason wet sanded all the parts and Denny taught him how to buff to a high gloss shine. In the entire process Jason only buffed through the paint in two small areas, and those were along inside edges, so Denny was able to touch them up so they couldn't be noticed.

The rest of the day was spent in the kitchen making things to take on the boat for their picnic the next day. Amazingly, Denny didn't transfer to his recliner and watch television while Jason worked. He wheeled himself out into the kitchen and helped.

Grandmother Judy's cookbook was once again a Godsend, Jason loved the book as most of the recipes had hand-written notes on them changing the ingredients, or the amounts of each ingredient to her tastes. This was especially handy for things that Jason had never made, including the potato salad.

Both Jason and Denny had loved her potato salad, and when Jason mentioned that he was dying to have it again, Denny was all for it. So once Jason had the potatoes boiled, Denny sat with a TV tray across his lap and peeled the skins off and diced the potatoes.

"How much do you suppose a pinch is?" Jason asked while reading what Grandmother Judy had written.

"A pinch?"

"Yeah, that's what she wrote." Jason laughed. "And she sure loved that measure as she used it a lot."

Denny thought a moment as the 'engineer' part of his brain kicked in. "I would assume that a pinch is what could be held between one's fingers. And since your hands are bigger than hers, I would venture to say that maybe ¾ a pinch of your hands would equal a full pinch of hers."

Jason just looked at his grandfather a moment, trying to determine if that had been a joke. "Really? You think so?"

"Well yeah," Denny replied. "Look at your hands, and then remember how small hers were?"

Jason just gave him a questioning look.

"Over-thinking it, am I?" Denny laughed.

"A bit."

Next Jason had to find a Tupperware bowl and lid big enough to hold all he had made of it. As he went through each and every drawer and cupboard in the kitchen. He found Tupperware in almost all of them, but nothing big enough to hold all the potato salad he was about to make.

"I can't believe that grandma had all this Tupperware and not one big enough to do the job for us." Jason said out of frustration.

"Oh, Tupperware was her only weakness." Denny laughed. "There has to be another place she kept the larger ones. I know she had them."

Tupperware was found in the hall closet, on shelves lining the sides of the basement stairs, and even a large plastic bag of it found in the basement. Jason was able to find the perfect bowl but couldn't find the lid. The search for a bowl and matching lid turned into a two-hour search.

"This winter, when we don't have anything better to do. We are going to spend a day matching this crap up." Denny said as he sat in his wheelchair looking at dozens of pieces of Tupperware and assorted lids.

“We might be better off to just throw it all out and start over.” Jason laughed. “I never knew she had so much stuff. She was like a hoarder of plastic bowls.”

Denny laughed while Jason got three tall kitchen plastic bags out and went about bagging all the pieces up. When everything had been collected and bagged, it was taken down to the basement to await that winter day when they found themselves bored to death.

Once Jason had the salad all mixed up, both tried it and smiled. “She is still with us.” Denny smiled a sad smile.

CHAPTER ELEVEN

Everyone was up early and by 8AM had the boat hooked up and were on their way to the public boat launch at the river.

Jason did an excellent job of backing the boat in and pulling back out once Hank had it launched.

The big question then was how to get Denny safely aboard. When they could find no suitable way of doing it, Jason had an idea. He unhooked the trailer from the Suburban and together with Hank placed Denny up on the tailgate. He then had Hank bring the boat in as close as he could while he backed the Suburban down into the water's edge.

Jason then removed his shoes and socks and rolled his pant legs up. While Hank and Issy took Denny's arms from the front of the boat, Jason helped lift him from the space between the boat and truck.

It almost worked too, until the boat drifted away from the truck and all four of them ended up in the water!

From there it was a comic mix of bad ideas until Issy finally said that they might as well try to land Denny as they would a big fish. She and Hank got back on the boat while Jason pushed up from the water. They finally succeeded in dragging Denny over the edge of the boat's deck until they had him onboard.

When Jason returned to the shore to move the truck, a handful of people had gathered to watch them. Why they hadn't offered any help passed through his mind, but instead of him getting the seats of the new truck wet by moving it himself. He asked one of the men standing there to do it for him.

The morning on the river was beautiful. What surprised them the most was that with such a beautiful day, only a few others were spotted on the water. They tried several nice spots that they thought would be good fishing, but nothing was caught.

Around noon they found a nice shady spot along the bank and anchored under massive old trees for their lunch. Before eating Issy insisted on saying a prayer.

Issy thanked God for the wonderful day and friends they could share it with. She also prayed for Denny's healing.

Then she finished the prayer with "If it be your will Lord, guide us to where the fish are."

Issy had made wonderful ham and egg salad sandwiches, which along with Jason's potato salad made a meal that pleased everyone. Issy and Hank kept complimenting Jason on how great the potato salad was while he and Denny exchanged winks.

While they were eating, a dead limb fell out of one of the trees and crashed to the ground with a loud pop. Both Hank and Denny instantly jerked and ducked their heads. Both men took deep breaths to calm their nerves while Jason and Issy exchanged knowing glances.

After they finished with lunch, the anchors were pulled up and they motored further down the river. The natural beauty of the river was so impressive that they couldn't believe all this wonder was so close to home and they hadn't enjoyed it long before this.

They had motored about a mile upriver when Issy noticed a very faded red cloth stuck to a large tree trunk that had fallen in the river. She had Hank steer as close to it as he could while Jason leaned over the side of the boat and grabbed it. The moment Issy looked the cloth over, she insisted that Hank stop the boat and drop anchor.

"Here?" Hank asked to be sure.

"This is the spot." Issy insisted.

While Hank and Jason were dropping the anchors, Issy stood up and looked about herself. Sure enough, about half a mile in the distance, she spotted an old red barn.

"Okay lady," Hank said to her. "We're at anchor. Want to explain why here?"

"See that old barn over there?" Issy pointed toward the barn.

"Yeah, it's an old barn. So?"

"You don't remember it?" Issy asked with a surprised tone of voice.

"Should I?" Hank was bewildered.

"We came fishing here many years ago." Issy explained. "Before we had Becky."

Hank was trying to remember but failed.

Issy turned a bit red, then whispered something to Hank.

"Skinny-dipping?" Hank asked, which made Issy's face turn beet red.

"Hank!" Issy scolded him, which made both Jason and Denny laugh. "You really don't remember."

"That's right!" It suddenly dawned on Hank's memory. "You forgot to remove your bandana and when you dove under the water, it slipped off and we couldn't find it."

"Right." Issy was pleased he finally remembered what was a priceless memory to her, "This big snag wasn't here then, but believe it or not, this is my long-lost bandana." She opened her hand so Hank could have a good look at the faded red cloth.

"No way! I mean how could you possibly know that that red cloth is the same one you had so many years ago?"

Issy turned the cloth so everyone could see the darker colored stitching along the edges. "See the edges of it. One side is gone now, but that darker stitching used to be black. There is no question in my mind that this old rag is what is left of my once favorite bandana."

"Okay. So, what does finding that old cloth mean to you?" Hank asked.

"As Jesus told the disciples when they weren't having any luck fishing. Here is where you cast."

The men were amazed by their turn in fortune. They suddenly found themselves landing fish with almost each cast. Most of the catches were Carp and Sucker fish, but more than ten beautiful Catfish were also caught. The catfish they kept while releasing the others.

That evening the four of them enjoyed fresh fried catfish and the balance of Jason's potato salad, topped off with some of Issy's amazing cookies.

While Jason helped get his grandfather into his night clothes and then into the recliner, he commented on the long-lost bandana and it marking the hot fishing spot.

"That is a tough one to explain." Denny agreed. "What do you make of it?"

"I'm not sure." Jason honestly replied. "When Bell was here, she told of answered prayers. How she believed that God, Jesus, or maybe a guardian angel was always looking out for us. What I can't fathom, is if that were true, why did my parents die?"

At first Denny didn't answer. A part of him wondered the same thing, then remembered something Judy had always said. "Their time was up. They had done what they were supposed to do, and they got to go home."

Jason looked at his grandfather for a moment. He hadn't heard those words since his grandmother had passed. "Grandma always said that very thing."

"That's who I was quoting."

"Do you believe it?" Jason asked.

"Not as much as she did." Denny admitted. "But it would explain things we don't understand. To be honest it would explain a lot of things I have seen over the course of my life. Both now, and in the military."

"What do you mean?"

"When I was in Vietnam, I was surrounded by others just like myself. I saw many of them meet their end. Sometimes it was a stupid mistake on their part, but often it was pure chance. A rocket would land in our midst, and I was just far enough away or shielded by other bodies that took the hit. The enemy was firing blind. Some died, others like me went uninjured."

Jason didn't respond. It was the most his grandfather had talked of his time in southeast Asia, he wanted him to say as much as he wanted to without interruption.

"It happened time and time again." Denny went on. "Those boys lost their lives, their hopes and dreams. Their parents lost their children. I didn't fully appreciate that until your parents were killed."

"You had gone to bed. Your grandmother and I were going through family pictures. With broken hearts and tears we revisited those special moments from the past. The silly things your father did as a toddler, the handsome and talented young man he became. Then when he started dating your beautiful mother. Their marriage, and your birth. We travelled through time with those photographs right up until our last Christmas together. It was the last pictures we had of them, they died just a month later. The worst part of all was that I never told your father that I loved him, that I was proud of him and that he meant the world to me."

"He knew." Jason assured him as tears ran down his face. "I refused to give my mom a hug and a kiss before leaving for school the day she died."

The two of them looked at each other with tears.

"So, what do I think happened today?" Denny forced a smile. "Issy prayed for a sign of where the fish were biting. That old faded red cloth resurfaced to do just that. Where it had been all those years, is beyond my ability to understand. I will tell you this. The entire life I had with your grandmother; she was always trying to make me believe her faith as she did. You may not believe this, but I talk to her all the time. Tell her how I miss her, loved her..." He paused a moment. "And tell her how proud she would be of you."

That made Jason smile.

"So, what I believe, is that our guardian angel may be your grandmother. It could also be your dad or mom. Maybe it is the Holy Spirit that she always talked about, but I never really understood. Either way, that cloth today was a sign that your grandmother knew I would notice and feel deep in my miserable heart."

"I don't think you have a miserable heart."

Denny smiled a sad smile. "For most of my life I sure have had. And what breaks my heart now is the possibility that your parents and Grandmother Judy's task in life was to change me. When the things like their love, their caring didn't do it, they paid the highest price of all."

"That's not true." Jason said with more force than he intended. "What if it isn't you at all, but me."

"You? Don't even think that." Denny scolded.

"Not in a bad way," Jason corrected. "But what if I am to do something with my life that will make a big difference. What if my parents' job was to get me to the point that I could be molded by you and grandmother?

What if when grandmother had done all she was supposed to do, she got to go home so you could take over. And if all of that was true, what if Heaven is as grandmother always said it was. What if this life, no matter how wonderful it is, is a horrible existence in comparison to Heaven? And if she was right about that, maybe she was also right that a day in Heaven is a lifetime here on earth. They will all still be unpacking by the time we join them."

"I honestly don't know about all of that." Denny said. "I can tell you that other things she used to say are true. Sometimes when something bad happens to us, it turns out to be the best thing that could possibly happen."

"Such as?" Jason asked.

"My leg for example." Denny replied instantly.

"I don't follow, how breaking your leg is the best thing that could have happened to you."

"Oh, but it was." Denny smiled. "If I hadn't broken my leg, we would have continued down that same old path. It took breaking my leg to open my eyes. For the first time since I left the military hospital, I couldn't do anything for myself. I had to rely on the charity of others. Namely you, but also Issy and Hank. Even then I didn't appreciate what all of you were doing for me. It took a dream about Grandma Judy and the smell of your cooking to finally pull the curtain back and let the light of life through."

The two talked well into the night, and both paid the price in the morning. They probably would have just slept in, but Denny needed to visit the Throne Room as he called it. And today was going to be assembly day in the shop.

CHAPTER TWELVE

Both Jason and Denny had a hard time getting motivated at first, but as the pieces started going together the excitement grew. By noon the bike was back together, and the side car firmly attached.

While they were eating their lunch, the man from the upholstery shop came by with the seat, backrest, head rest, and canopy cover. The seat had been done in an antique white with a deep red piping that came close to matching the main color of the bike. The canopy, which snapped in place over the side car was of that same deep red color.

After Denny wrote the man a check and he had left, both just stared at their creation. It was far and away the sharpest bike Denny had ever built.

“Let’s get it out into the sun.” Denny said.

Jason was nervous at first, but as soon as he was out of the shop, he did a few figure eights in the back yard before parking it in the direct sunlight.

As he was walking back into the shop, he spotted both Hank and Issy headed their way. By the time he had Denny out to the bike, they were standing next to it admiring it.

"That is absolutely the most beautiful bike I have ever seen." Issy told them. "You two are amazing."

"I couldn't agree more." Hank added.

"Thank you." Denny replied. "But Jason here gets most of the credit. He did most of the work on the sidecar and did all of the painting."

"I couldn't have done any of it without you. You coached me every step of the way." Jason corrected him.

"What is something like this worth?" Issy asked.

Denny tossed out a rough price range.

"Really?" Hank asked. "That is less than I would have thought."

"You think that you might want a bike?" Denny asked. "That price was for strangers. I could do a lot better for the two of you."

"Oh, we have spent more than we should in the last week." Issy laughed nervously. She could see the look on Hank's face.

"Wanting and being able to own are two very different things." Hank replied.

"Still have your bike license?" Denny asked.

"Of course." Hank replied.

"Why don't you take Issy for a ride?" Denny suggested, as he told Jason to remove the side car canopy.

"Oh, we can't do that." Issy told him.

"Sure, you can." Denny laughed. "Let Jason help you into the side car."

"If we take it for a ride, you're going to want it." Issy said to Hank.

"I already want it." Hank admitted. "Taking it for a ride won't change anything."

Once Issy was in the sidecar and Hank was sitting on the bike but hadn't started it yet, Denny cautioned him. "Driving a bike with a sidecar is a lot different than riding a bike. You really are driving more than riding. You must turn into corner, not lean into them. You also always must keep the width of the sidecar in mind. So just take it slowly at first until you get the hang of it."

The ride was a thrill for both Hank and Issy. As they were going around the neighborhood, Issy couldn't believe how many people stopped and watched them go by. Some waved, gave the thumbs up, or just pointed them out to others nearby.

When they got back to the shop Jason helped Issy from the sidecar as Hank and Denny talked about the bike.

Jason led Issy over to the two lawn chairs sitting under the maple tree. They talked about the bike for a couple of minutes, then Jason had a serious question for her.

"How do you pray?" Jason simply asked, after not being able to find another way of putting it.

"How do I pray?" Issy asked to be sure she understood what he had asked. While also giving her a moment to think of her answer.

"Yes, how do you pray?" Jason repeated the question. "I have seen my parents pray, Grandmother Judy pray, and I watched you pray. It seems so natural and easy, and yet I can't seem to feel like I am doing it right."

Issy reached out and took his hand in hers. "Did you ever have trouble talking to your father when you were growing up?"

"Only when I was in trouble." Jason smiled.

"That was when you needed to talk to him the most, wasn't it?"

Jason smiled and nodded his head.

"Your father was your earthly father. He was the father of your body. God is your Heavenly Father, and Father of your soul. Talk to God as you would your earthly father. Be honest, be open, and believe that he truly loves you as your earthly father had also loved you."

Is it that simple?" Jason was having a hard time absorbing what she was telling him.

"Talking with God is truly the easiest conversation you can possibly have with anyone." Issy smiled. "He already knows your heart. He hears your silent prayers, and fully understands your needs, wants, and desires even before you do."

"Really?"

"God loves us as any parent would love their child. He created us and then, as any parent will do, set down rules for us to follow. When we didn't follow the rules, he still loved us so much that he gave us Jesus who took on our sins and wrongful ways and shed his blood on the cross for us. It is through Jesus that we have a way to be welcomed back into the family of God, even when we don't deserve it."

"What about the rituals of prayer?"

"Rituals?" Issy wondered what he meant.

"Yeah, like bowing your head, kneeling, putting your hands together." Jason answered.

"Ah, the rituals." Issy smiled. "When you are at a time and place where you can do that, you should. It is showing respect for your Heavenly Father. Sometimes, however, you will need help when you can't do those things. God understands, he knows your heart. Call out to him in Jesus's name and he will hear your plea. What is more important to God than the rituals, as you call them, is what is in your heart."

By this time the men had concluded their conversation over at the bike and were headed their way. Jason got up and offered his chair to Hank.

"Did you?" Issy inquired of Hank.

"No, not at this time. The truck and boat took all I can spend for now."

Issy just nodded her understanding.

"Denny did make an attractive offer though."

“Oh” Issy was afraid to ask.

“Hank said that you two used to ride all the time, before his legs got a bit unstable.” Denny said. “With a sidecar, you don’t have to hold the bike up at stop signs and such. So, if you two would enjoy it, when my leg is healed, and I am strong enough to do so again. I will let you two take the bike with the sidecar. I’ll take one of my other bikes, and Jason can keep up with his bike, so we can all go for a cruise on the bikes.”

“Really?” Issy liked that idea. “But we can’t take your beautiful bike.”

“Why not?” Denny asked. “Issy, you have done more than you know to help Jason and myself. Loaning you the bike for a brief cruise is the least that I could do for you and Hank.”

Issy smiled and reached over and patted Denny’s arm. “It is what neighbors and friends do for one another.”

“That may well be,” Denny said. “But dear lady, you have gone above and beyond. My grandson and I owe you so much for all you have done for us. You have touched our hearts and minds in ways I’ll never be able to explain.”

Issy got up out of her chair and stepped over to Denny and bent down and gave him a hug in his chair. Then she turned and hugged Jason as well. "If I helped you, you're welcome. I will tell you that I could only do so much, the rest was up to the two of you. I am proud of what you two have accomplished." Then she smiled and pointed back at the bike. "And that wonderfully beautiful machine is the least of what the two of you have done in recent weeks."

That night while Jason was making supper, Denny had followed him to the kitchen in his wheelchair. While he worked, Jason told his grandfather about his talk with Issy about God and prayer.

"Could it be that simple?" Denny wondered.

Jason turned from the stove and looked at Denny. "There is one big issue that comes before dealing with how easy prayer is."

"And that is?"

"Belief." Jason answered. "A pure and simple, but total belief."

Denny thought about that for a bit. "Do you believe?"

Jason shrugged. “I think so. You?”

“I think so as well.” Denny answered. “These recent events in our lives are simply too much to just explain away. I am beginning to see what your Grandmother Judy could always see.”

“Yeah.” Jason agreed. “It’s funny, but I feel it as well. I can’t explain the feeling, but it is there, and I feel it.”

That night, as they got the food set up on Denny’s workstation in the shop because that was the easiest place for him to sit at and eat. Before they dished up their plates, they looked at each other. Denny smiled and reached out his right hand for Jason’s left.

They bowed their heads and for the first time in his entire life, Denny spoke to God in front of someone else. He gave thanks for all the blessings that had been showered upon them. At the end of the prayer, Denny asked God for another shop project if it was his will.

CHAPTER THIRTEEN

The next two days were spent cleaning and organizing the shop. Something that Denny explained always had to be done after a project. The main topic of conversation during the day and at their evening meal was faith.

At the end of the second day, there was nothing more they could do to make the shop more organized. A lot of that was due to the many tools, parts, and bits and pieces that Denny insisted be kept.

With nothing to look forward to doing the next day, Denny offered to treat Jason to dinner out. They decided on the same steak buffet that they both liked and had frequented often.

They were a couple of blocks from the restaurant when Denny suddenly asked Jason to stop the car. He then looked like he was trying to turn around in his seat.

"What?" Jason asked in total confusion.

"Get turned around." Denny instructed. "I think God just answered another prayer."

Jason did as he was instructed and turned the car around at a gas station at the end of the street. Driving slowly back the way he had come to allow Denny to find whatever he thought he had seen.

"Pull over." Denny quickly instructed. "Pull over."

Jason parked the car at the curb and looked around and didn't spot anything.

"See the black van parked at that brown house?" Denny asked.

"Yeah." Jason replied. "So what?"

"What I want to see is parked behind that van. Please get my wheelchair out."

Jason did as he was told and didn't spot what his grandfather was talking about until they were nearly upon the van. Partially covered with a silver plastic tarp was an old pickup truck.

Jason wheeled his grandfather as close to the old truck as he could get him. Denny asked Jason to go and knock on the house door while he looked the old truck over.

Jason was greeted at the door by a young mother holding a fussy baby in dire need of a bath. "Hello, do you own the old truck?"

“My husband does.” The lady replied while trying to quiet the child. “I’ll send him out.”

“Thank you.” Jason said as he turned and went back to where his grandfather was. In a couple of minutes, the young man joined them at the truck.

“Is your truck for sale?” Denny asked.

“I hadn’t planned on selling it.” The young man replied. “But we got some unexpected bills and money is tight. What are you willing to pay?”

“Well, I don’t know.” Denny replied. “Can you uncover it so I can see it better. And maybe back the van up a bit so I can get around the truck better.”

“Sure.” The young man replied, and quickly pulled the old tarp off the truck. Then he ran into the house and got the keys to back the van up.

While he was doing that, Denny had Jason checking out the cab corners and floors. All appeared to be solid.

“I was told that it was a one-owner truck from west Texas.” The man explained. “I was like the third person to buy it since it got to Michigan.”

“Does it run?”

“It does but has a lower end noise I can’t figure out.” Came the reply.

"It's a 1957, right?"

"It is." The man replied.

"How much do you have to get out of it?" Denny asked.

"It only has 54,000 miles showing, but I am not sure if the odometer works." The man replied. "I need to get $2,500.00 out of it."

Denny thought a moment. "I can't do that. It is a pretty old truck with a bad engine. I can give you $1,500.00 cash for it."

"No, I can't." The young man replied shaking his head. By this time his wife and baby had joined them. "The least I can take is $2,000.00."

Denny thought that over a second. "Okay, I understand. Thank you for letting us look at it." He turned his chair around and nodded his head at Jason to head for their car.

As they started walking away, Jason noticed the young mother go up to her husband and start whispering something that he couldn't hear.

Denny and Jason had almost made it to the street when the young man called them back. Jason turned Denny's wheelchair around and pushed him back up to the front of the old truck.

"I think it is worth more, but we really need the money. Cash right."

"Cash." Denny agreed. "We're going to get something to eat right now. Then we'll go home and get the money and come back."

"Any way you could get the money first?" The young man asked. "We're out of money and need some groceries."

Denny looked at Jason, who shrugged signaling that it was okay with him. "We'll do that. Got a clean title?"

"I sure do. In my name too." The young man reached out and shook Denny's hand.

"It takes me a bit to get around, so give us an hour." Denny said.

"That'll be fine."

Once they got back home and Jason got Denny into the house, he was sent next door to ask Hank to come over.

Jason and Hank were back to the house as Denny wheeled himself out of his bedroom.

"Jason tells me that you bought an old truck." Hank said as Denny came into the living room.

"I did." Denny replied. "Care to give us a hand in towing it back here?"

"Sure." Hank smiled. "I'll go throw some chains in the back of the suburban and we'll go get it."

"No, let's use my car." Denny countered. "I already have a couple of chains in it, and we don't know how good the brakes are on that old truck. If it is going to bump into something, better my old car than that new truck of yours."

"You want me to steer the old truck?" Hank asked.

"I want you to drive my car, the tow vehicle. I think that is tougher to do than steering the old truck. Jason can handle that part of the deal."

When they got back to the house, the young man had moved his van out of the way. While Denny was paying for the truck and getting the title signed off, Hank and Jason hooked the old truck to the back of Denny's car with about 20 feet of chain between them.

Before taking off for home Denny explained what Jason was to do. "Try to keep the chain tight. It won't be easy but do your best. When you see the brake lights come on, you apply the truck brakes. Then it is a simple matter of keeping it straight behind us and following us home.

Jason was nervous and allowed a couple of hard jerks, but about half of the way home he seemed to get the hang of it. In less than thirty minutes they pulled into the driveway. Denny had Hank pull as close to the garage as he could before turning into the yard to get it even closer, while signaling Jason to point the truck toward the garage.

Denny offered to treat Hank and Issy to supper for his help, but they had already eaten. Two and a half hours after they had set out for the restaurant Denny and Jason finally got there.

Over supper they talked about the project before them. They would get it to the shop somehow, and then pull the engine. They could either get a remanufactured one or find a good one in a salvage yard. It would all come down to price and what they found available.

The following morning all three of them gathered around the truck. Denny told them that the engine was bad anyway, but he wanted to hear it, so after blocking the wheels, Hank started the truck. Amazingly, it started right up and other than a loud clunking noise, it ran pretty smooth.

Even with Hank's help, moving the truck into the shop proved to be more than they could handle, so Denny had Jason and Hank bring the cherry-picker, a portable one-armed hoist on strong extended legs out to the front of the garage.

Hank and Jason followed Denny's directions and removed the hood, drained the coolant and oil. Next came removal of the battery, the starter and generator and anything else connected to the engine.

The actual removal of the engine went quickly once they had the bolts connecting it to the bellhousing removed. Even with draining all the fluids beforehand, the engine leaked a lot of coolant and oil onto the driveway.

"Good thing your grandmother isn't here to see this mess." Denny laughed. "Go into the house and bring out a box of Tide."

"Laundry soap?" Jason asked to be sure.

"Yes, it is quite good at cleaning this kind of mess off of concrete." Denny said.

Then he noticed a couple of short but thick bolts laying on the ground under the truck. "Grab those bolts first." He told Jason.

When Jason handed the bolts to Denny, his grandfather turned them over a couple of times in his hand. "It might not be the engine that is bad." Denny said, as he wheeled himself over to the back of the engine hanging from the hoist.

While Jason went after the soap, Hank removed the bolts from the pressure plate and then the clutch unit. Three bolts were missing from the flywheel. Marks inside the bellhousing showed him where the loose bolts were getting caught on the clutch plate or flywheel and being thrown around inside the bellhousing. Both of the bolts Jason had picked up off the ground were well beaten and scarred.

The clutch kit itself looked to be fairly new, which told Denny that whoever had replaced it, had not torqued the bolts properly, or had lost the lock washers.

He gave the beat-up bolts to Jason and sent him down to the local parts store to get new ones with lock washers.

By the end of the day, the engine was back in the truck, and everything connected back up. This time when Hank fired the engine up there wasn't any noise coming from it. The loose bolts had indeed been the only problem.

This time when Denny offered to take Hank and Issy to supper, they agreed. Before they left the house, Denny went back into his bedroom and didn't come back out for five minutes. On the way to the restaurant Denny had Hank stop at the house where they had bought the truck. Denny had Jason wheel him up close to the front steps, and then knocked on the door.

This time, both the young man and his wife came to the door. "I'm sorry sir, I can't refund your money." The young man said.

"I didn't come for a refund." Denny smiled. "The repair to the truck was less costly than I had envisioned so I want to give you your full asking price."

Both the young couple and Jason were surprised as Denny handed a thousand dollars over to the young couple. "You have a young family to take care of, and I am happy paying the full price." Denny smiled and shook the young man's hand.

As they turned to leave, the young mother bent over Denny and gave him a hug. Which almost had the baby in his lap.

She was crying as she told Denny how much his honesty meant to them. They were having a hard time financially and the extra money was an answer to their prayers.

With the young mother's tears smeared across Denny's face, he and Jason turned and headed back to Hank's suburban. "Why did you do that?" Jason asked.

"I don't really know." Denny honestly replied. "All I can say is that when I realized that the engine didn't have to be replaced, I felt something very strong in my heart. I knew I had to do this."

"Grandma Judy?" Jason wondered out loud.

"Our guardian angel." Denny laughed. "The lady did say that it was an answer to their prayers. So, my guess is that it was indeed your grandmother. Whenever she felt I needed to learn a lesson, she went about it without subtlety. And she would drive her point home numerous times to be sure I got the message."

CHAPTER FOURTEEN

The next morning, they had gotten the title transferred and a set of license plates and insurance. Jason helped Denny up into the passenger side of the truck while he got behind the wheel. The day would be spent learning to drive a stick shift.

Every day the two set out on little trips and enjoyed venturing out into the country. By the end of the week Jason could drive the truck and shift without even thinking about it.

The following week was a busy one. Denny's cast was removed and a harder, stiffer one put on. This one he would be able to put a little pressure on.

Bell was back from her mission trip and planned on spending a week with her grandparents. Jason got to spend a lot of time with her and gave her rides on his bike and in the old truck, both of which she loved. Three of the days were spent out on the river fishing and enjoying the natural beauty of the river.

For each day's picnic Jason made something special from Grandma Judy's cookbook. One day he offered to bring the meat part of the picnic and surprised everyone with tacos. He had packed everything in a Styrofoam cooler that he had first washed out with hot water. Then he lined the inside of the cooler with foil and placed a folded towel in the bottom of the cooler. He wrapped all the hot food items twice in foil and placed them on top of the towel before folding a second towel and placing it on top of the food.

Everyone seemed to enjoy the tacos, especially Bell. What surprised them even more was Jason saying the prayer before they ate. As Issy had done, he prayed for good fishing and for God to show them where to fish.

While the adults fished from under the boat's canopy, Jason and Bell took a couple of folding chairs and sat out on the boat's bow to fish. Unlike the day Issy had prayed for good fishing, this day it didn't happen. Everyone had a few bites every now and then. Bell and Jason caught the most with a couple of fish each. Nothing they wanted to keep so all were released back into the river.

While they sat in the sun waiting for a bite Jason commented. "I guess I am not as good at praying as your grandmother is."

Bell laughed at that. "Maybe we're just suppose to enjoy this beautiful day."

"Maybe." Jason frowned.

"I was impressed with your prayer." Bell said. "It sounded heart-felt, and when talking to God we must always mean what we say because he knows if we don't."

"Makes sense." Jason replied.

"I also loved the tacos." Bell smiled. "Tacos are a favorite food of mine."

"What else do you like to eat?"

"I love almost everything." Bell laughed. "Except maybe eggplant and a couple of other disgusting foods. I also don't like to put too much in the way of sauces on my food. I want the true taste of the food to come through."

"I'm the same way." Jason agreed.

"You are pretty amazing." Bell suddenly said. "Not many guys your age can do so many different things and do them all so well."

Jason blushed at that. "Thanks, but I have had the best teachers. Especially your grandmother."

"She enjoys you too." Bell said with a laugh. "She said you were the best student she ever had, which includes me."

When they got the boat back to Hank and Issy's, Bell helped her grandmother make dinner while the men washed and covered the boat. They had a little picnic out under Denny's big maple tree and as before, the adults talked while Bell and Jason sat a bit apart from them so they could talk.

"When do you have to go back to school?" Jason asked.

"Right after Labor Day." Bell replied. "And you?"

"Same." Jason replied.

"This summer has really passed quickly." Bell said. "Maybe because I think it may be the best summer I have ever had."

"Really?" Jason asked. "I would have to agree with that. When the school year was about over last spring, I wasn't even looking forward to the summer, but it turned out incredible."

Bell looked at him with her piercing blue eyes and a soft smile. "Yes, it has."

They talked about all the miraculous things that had happened between Jason and his grandfather, and about Bell's mission trip. When the conversation started to lag Bell changed the subject.

"My grandparents were talking about taking a trip with you and your grandfather on the motorcycles if his leg heals in time."

"Yeah, that would be cool."

"It sure would be." Bell sounded like she was hoping to be invited.

"If we can, are you coming along?" Jason asked.

"You think I could? I would love to." Bell was excited, but suddenly frowned. "But I don't have a bike, how would I be able to come along?"

"All three of the bikes have a passenger seat." Jason pointed out.

"Your bike does too?"

"It does." Jason assured her. "Not made for anyone too big, but for you and me, it would be great."

"Really?" The excitement was back in Bell's voice. "I sure hope we can do it. That would truly cap off the best summer I have ever had as well."

With only two weeks before school was scheduled to start Denny finally got the cast off his leg. He was to wear a strap-on brace for as long as he felt he needed it. True to form, Denny didn't bother with the strap-on brace for the first day. It wasn't until his leg felt really sore that he even tried it. Surprisingly, the brace didn't bother his walking or getting on his bike, and it did support the leg lessening the pain. From then on, the brace was strapped on every morning.

The first thing Denny wanted to do when the cast came off was get back on his bike. He did sit on it, and when he pulled it up off the kick stand, he realized that he needed to build the strength in the leg before he would be ready to ride again.

With nothing in the shop to work on, Denny and Jason would go for walks each morning and then again in the afternoon. Each day the walks became longer and longer. By the end of the week, he was back on his bike and riding for hours each day. Most of his rides stayed in town where he would have to stop at lights and stop signs. Before they took a trip of any length, he wanted to be sure he was up to it.

Finally, on Friday afternoon, Denny and Jason walked over to Hank and Issy's. Together they made plans for the trip they had looked forward to for so long. They had come up with a plan to first ride to South Haven and then follow the Lake Michigan coast to Traverse City, then over to Petoskey and follow Michigan Route 119 north through "the tunnel of trees" and spend the night in Mackinaw City. The trip home would be following the Lake Huron coastline south and then back up into the thumb area, before turning back south and riding to Port Huron.

Everyone liked the plan, and when Jason asked if Bell would be coming, Issy was surprised she hadn't thought to call her. She excused herself and went and made that call. When she came to the table, she was smiling. She had heard that Denny's cast had come off and had already started packing for the trip.

Denny laughed. "You did remind her that it was a motorcycle trip, so space for luggage will be limited."

"I did." Issy laughed. "She wanted to know what limited meant exactly."

The plan was to pull out early Sunday morning, so Bell's parents dropped her off at her grandparents' Saturday afternoon. Even knowing that luggage space was limited, Bell had packed way too much to fit on the bikes. Issy spent the afternoon helping her go through her clothes and picking out what could and could not be taken. It came down to seven pairs of socks and underwear, three tops and two sets of jeans, a coat and a set of gloves in case the weather got cool.

Sunday dawned cool and gray. The weather forecast was for lower-than-normal temps and scattered rain showers. Before climbing on the bikes, Issy had them all join hands and she said a prayer for safety, for good riding conditions and gave thanks for the opportunity for them to rejoice in friendship and love.

The trip to South Haven took roughly two hours. Twice they ran into light rain but by the time they parked the bikes on the beach at South Haven the sky had started to clear, and the sun had warmed things back up.

As they headed north following the lake shore as much as they could, it turned into a truly beautiful day. Jason had to smile to himself. He had grown very fond of Bell, and she had chosen to ride with him. He liked having her arms around him. This was going to be a memorable trip indeed.

Twice along the way to Traverse City, they stopped along the side of the road and walked down paths cut through the six-foot tall sand dunes lining the lake's shore. Everyone removed their shoes and socks and walked along the water's edge with the waves rolling over their feet as they went.

Because of the many stops along their route, the group decided to spend the first night on the road in Traverse City. They found a nice mom-pop run motor lodge.

The next day was no different. They made numerous stops along the way before reaching Petoskey. Stopping for lunch and a little shopping, Issy and Bell were both warned that if they bought too much, something would have to be left behind. Then it was north on Michigan route 119 and after about ten miles they came to what is known as 'the tunnel of trees" which is a winding road running right alongside of Lake Michigan. The winding road is completely covered with an almost solid canopy of trees.

It was nearly dusk by the time they finally reached Mackinaw City at the very tip of Michigan's lower peninsula. They first found rooms for the night and then went downtown to enjoy some shopping and a place to have dinner.

The Adults went back to the hotel while Jason and Bell went down to the small public beach on the shores of the Mackinaw Strait. There they found a place to sit down and gaze upon the brightly illuminated 5-mile-long Mackinaw Bridge. They talked of many things, but mostly about how they saw their future.

"Have you come up with what you want to study when you go to college" Bell asked him.

"Well, after this summer, I think it might in in engineering." Jason replied.

"Had a good summer, huh?"

"The most amazing summer of my life." Jason laughed.

"How so?" Bell was intrigued.

"So much happened this summer that I can hardly believe it myself." Jason started. "If you had told me that my life would do a complete 180 in just a matter of a few months, I would never have believed you. And it isn't just one aspect of my life, but almost everything is different now than it was just a few months ago. And not just my life, but my grandfather's as well."

"My grandfather is far more open and communitive than he had ever been as well." Bell injected. "Even grandmother says so."

Jason nodded. "The biggest factors in bringing all this change about was first losing my grandmother, then grandfather breaking his leg, which brought us to our lowest point. Then your grandparents stepped in, especially your Grandmother Issy. She stepped in at our lowest point and guided us through it. Teaching us what we needed to do to get through it. More importantly, she taught us about her faith."

Bell listened silently, just watching Jason tell his story. She thought he was very good looking, smart and communicated well, even if he always used his hands while he talked. She liked him a lot.

Jason told her everything that had happened, and how that changed things for the better in his life. When told of the red scarf being found, Bell couldn't believe it. And laughed when Jason told her that her grandparents had lost the scarf when they went skinny-dipping in the river.

The following day, they decided to make a small change in their travel plans and crossed the Mackinaw bridge and rode to the oldest city in Michigan and the third oldest city in the United States, Sault Ste. Marie.

They had lunch at a crazy restaurant called The Antlers sitting amongst dozens of stuff animals, bomb casings and various other oddities. Then they did a little shopping and spent time watching the huge Great Lakes freighters locking through the Soo Locks.

By mid-afternoon they were ready to head south again and found a cozy log cabin motel just north of St. Ignace. After checking in they went downtown and visited numerous gift stores and some of the historical museums.

The following morning, they set out heading south on Michigan Route 23 following the Lake Huron coast. The plan was to hook up with route 25 just outside of Bay City and follow it around the bottom of Saginaw Bay and then north into the thumb. They had planned on spending the night at Port Austin at the northern end of the thumb, but there were just too many antique stores and other interesting attractions along the way. They ended up finding a less than desirable hotel just north of Bay City.

The ride from there to Port Austin was a leisurely one and they arrived there in the early afternoon. Here they found a quaint little family run motel right on the shore. As had happened at almost every stop, the adults enjoyed refreshments while Jason and Bell went down to the water's edge and talked.

"This is the best vacation I have ever had." Bell announced.

"I think so too." Jason agreed. "What makes it so for you?"

"Everything." Bell replied with a laugh. "Our state is so beautiful. The weather has blessed us, and I love doing it all on motorcycles. You feel more a part of everything. There are smells you miss in a car. Like when we went through the Tunnel of Trees. I could smell the trees, the forest all mixed with the smell of the Lake Michigan shoreline."

Jason nodded his head in agreement.

"What about you, what makes this the best trip ever?" Bell asked.

"You pretty much nailed it." Jason laughed. "Not much I could add."

The next morning after breakfast they headed south on Michigan route 25 and would follow the Lake Huron coast all the way to Port Huron. They arrived in Port Huron earlier than they had expected. Partly because they were at the point that they had no more storage on the bikes for trinkets, so they were no longer stopping at all the antique and craft stores.

After a bite to eat, they decided that it was too late to make the run for home but seemed too early to call it a day. Then Denny asked them how they felt about riding about half the way home before stopping for the night. That way they would get home before noon the next day. He also hinted that he had one more surprise they might enjoy.

Eager to learn what that surprise might be, Jason and Bell agreed instantly, which made Hank and Issy laugh. "Lead the way." Hank motioned at Denny.

They took Interstate 69 out of Port Huron and travelled west until they came to Michigan Route 23 south. Then when they came to Route 36 west Denny motioned for them to follow. Shortly after they came to a small town named Pinckney. Here they stopped for fuel and potty breaks.

"Where are you taking us?" Bell wanted to know.

"Someplace you will remember." Was all Denny would say.

"Is it very far?"

"Not far at all, but we need to be sure to have enough fuel to get us to where we can stop for the night." Denny replied.

"We won't be staying at this place?" Issy asked.

"No," Denny laughed. "And you'll probably be glad of that."

"What?" Both Bell and Issy seemed intrigued.

"You'll see when we get there." Denny laughed as he got back on his motorcycle.

They turned south in the middle of the small town, and it didn't take very long before Denny's right turn signal came on and then the brake light. They turned west on a road called Patterson Lake Road and in minutes rolled to a stop at little more than a single store.

"Where are we?" Issy asked as she slowly climbed up and out of the side car.

"Welcome to Hell." Denny laughed.

"What?" Bell asked as if she hadn't heard him correctly.

"We're in Hell, Michigan." Jason told her. "I suppose that now you can say that I would go to Hell and back with you."

That made Bell laugh, but she also liked that he had said that.

Issy was finally standing between the bikes. "Well, you were right about one thing."

"What's that?" Denny was all smiles.

"This isn't a place I want to stay."

The small store also served as a museum of sorts, and they found a sign with the history of the town inside.

It was settled around 1830, and then became official on October 13, 1841. According to legend, the name came from two German immigrants that made the comment "So Schön hell" which translates into "so beautifully bright". The locals that heard them didn't understand anything but the word Hell, and the name stuck.

The sun was setting in the west when they left Hell and headed southwest to Chelsea and found a room for the night.

Once they had their rooms, they found a family style restaurant for dinner. After they ordered the food, they talked and reflected on what everyone felt was a glorious vacation.

"It was far more than I had thought it would be." Bell said. "So much beauty and fun. It was also symbolic of how we don't want our lives to go."

"Beg your pardon?" Issy asked with a questioning look.

"Well," Bell giggled. "We started off in South Haven and ended up in Hell." Which made everyone laugh, even those at the table next to theirs.

The next morning dawned much cooler with a dark gray sky. They only had about a two-hour ride to get home, and after checking the forecast, which called for rain off and on for the next three days, they decided to head out and hopefully get home before it hit. Before jumping on Interstate 94, Denny explained how he handled riding in bad weather.

"If it starts to rain while we're riding, we'll slow down a bit. The road is slickest at first rain as the water is washing the oil off the pavement. If the rain is light and steady, we will keep riding. If any of you feel we need to pull off, honk your horn three times. That will be my signal to take the first exit we come to or stop under the next over-pass."

"If we pull off under an over-pass. We grab what we need and climb over the guardrail and away from the edge of the road. Remember, if a car is seeking shelter under the over-pass as well, it is because they are having trouble seeing in the rain and may not see our bikes in time. So, it's best if we're not standing next to them."

The light rain started just before they reached Jackson and continued all the way through town. Once they were past Jackson it let up for a few minutes and then suddenly the wind picked up and the rain started falling much harder. Hank was on his horn instantly. They pulled under the first over-pass they came to, and Denny took them to the far western edge of it before parking.

As soon as Denny and Hank had Issy out of the sidecar, they climbed the steep concrete abutment and took a seat. Of the five of them, Issy was the only one still dry. She commented on how water-tight the sidecar seemed to be.

The rain lasted for over an hour and the wind whipping through where they sat kept everyone chilled. Bell seemed to be feeling the worst of it as she had taken to shivering. Jason wrapped his arm around her, but it didn't seem to help much. Denny came up with an idea. They would get some of Bell's dry clothes out of the saddle bags. She would then get into the sidecar and change out of her wet things. Issy helped her into the sidecar and stood watch over it as Bell changed clothes. The dry clothes made a world of difference.

When the rain turned into a light drizzle, Denny said that they should probably get going. They had a little less than an hour to ride, so it was likely that they would hit rain again before getting home. Issy offered the sidecar to Bell, but she wanted to stay with Jason.

From the time they got home to Thanksgiving, they had so much to do. The trees around both yards decided to drop their leaves in thirds about a week apart, so both yards had to be raked three times. Then Denny and Jason helped Hank winterize the boat and get it securely covered for the winter.

Jason was now in his Junior year of High School and decided to play football. He did well, but never made the starting line-up. Unlike his time in school before, this year Jason made a lot of friends, some closer than others.

He also paid closer attention in class and his grades improved. He had always loved history class, but this year he found his true love was shop class. The teacher noticed how gifted Jason seemed to be and how he reveled in what the other classmates complained about. This led to discussions between Jason and the teacher about how to make things. The teacher was a big help in the drafting part of the process. Over the course of that school year Jason gained a lot of insight regarding drawing blueprints.

Since Hank and Issy would be all packed and ready to leave for Florida, Denny invited them over for Thanksgiving dinner. They thanked him but said that they were going to their daughter Becky's.

Being just the two of them didn't stop Jason from re-creating the feast they had had for Grandma Judy's last Thanksgiving with them. Over the meal they talked, laughed, and rejoiced in what an incredible year it had been. The Lord had seen them through the worst of times, to the best of times and both had learned a great deal. The biggest lesson Denny felt they had learned was to appreciate what they had. Great or small, things could always be worse.

CHAPTER FIFTEEN

The school year went by quickly. Jason took a very nice girl to the Junior prom. They had a fun time but when Jason didn't ask her out on a date later, she wasn't very nice to him.

Another project that Jason had been secretly working on was one that he felt would really mean a great deal to both his grandfather and Hank. He had no clue how he would go about it, but he was determined to find someone he had never met; Stanley Jenkins.

It was common for Jason to stop by the library on his way home. He had gotten to know the ladies that worked there, and they were so incredibly helpful when it came to research. The one lady Jason felt closest to was the least attractive of the three. She was as wide as she was tall, had totally unruly hair, wore thick horn-rimmed glasses, and clothes that had gone out of style a couple of fashion cycles ago.

She made up for all those shortcomings with a personality to match her size. She had a sharp wit, and quick mind. Above all these qualities, she possessed a heart of pure love.

When he hadn't gotten anywhere in his search for Sgt. Jenkins, he turned to Mrs. Coats, or Abbey, as she repeatedly told him to call her.

She listened to what he had to say, then turned around and grabbed a book off the shelf behind her counter. After leafing through it she stopped and wrote out an address on a sheet of paper.

Then she led Jason over to a set of typewriters and told him to write a letter to the name she had written on the paper. He did as she asked and when finished handed it to her so she could read it.

"Okay." Abbey said. "Nice try, but this time put your heart into it. Tell him why you are looking for this man. Explain to him that he can first check with Mr. Jenkins to see if your meeting him would be all right? But write a letter with some heart in it. Write a letter that will inspire action."

The second attempt was much better and met with Abbey's approval. "Now, tell him that you want this to be a secret, so he can reach you through me here at the library. And leave me your phone number so I can contact you if I hear something."

As soon as Jason had the letter written, Abbey placed it in an official Library envelope, and it went out in the morning's mail.

A response to his letter didn't come for almost two months. It wasn't until the last week of school that Abbey called, and Denny answered the phone since Jason hadn't made it home from school yet. She explained who she was and told Denny to ask Jason to return a book he had borrowed from the library.

When Jason did get home and his grandfather told him what the lady on the phone had said, Jason was confused. Then he remembered Abbey's plan. He did his best to act forgetful and rushed back out to his bike and headed off to the library.

When Jason walked into the library Abbey was busy with another patron, but she had seen him come in. When she finished with what she was doing, she went back into her cubical and retrieved the letter and handed it to Jason.

The letter was from the Pentagon and addressed to him in care of Abby at the library. The letter was rather formal but did say that it was wonderful that the two men could meet the man responsible for saving their lives. It went on to say that the Army had contacted Sgt. Jenkins regarding this matter, and he would enjoy having the men stop and see him. It finished off by giving all the contact information for Sgt. Jenkins.

Jason was beyond excited. He gave Abbey a big tight hug and kissed her cheek. “Miss Abbey, you have no idea how much this is going to mean to them.”

Half the people in the small Library had seen what had just taken place, making Abbey blush. “Glad I could help.”

The last day of school for the year, Jason took the truck to school so he could clean out his locker. After putting everything into the truck he went back in and spent a moment with each of his teachers thanking them for a good year. He did save his favorite for last, Clarence Bennet, the shop teacher. They talked for more than an hour at the end of which, Jason invited him to stop by sometime and see the kind of work that his grandfather and he did in the house shop.

Denny had taken on a couple of projects for the summer, but neither had a deadline, nor were they the type of projects that would require a great deal of time.

The neighbors were back home from Florida and by the time they had gotten home, Jason and Denny had their yard looking great.

Almost every weekend was spent doing small bike trips or out on the river. Jason asked about a bike road trip for this year, but no one seemed to know where they wanted to go. Jason suggested they should try going to some place they had never been before. While the three adults liked that idea, nothing was set in stone.

The second week of summer vacation started with Bell coming to spend a week with her grandparents. Jason and she spent a little time each day together. One evening Jason took her to the local Dairy Queen for a treat. While they were enjoying their ice cream, he told her about what he had in mind for the summer bike trip.

"Well, wait until I get back from our mission this year to Haiti."

"I don't want to go without you." Jason teased but meant it as well.

"You better not." Bell laughed.

"The problem is getting them to agree to go to Washington, Louisiana without telling them why." Jason lamented.

Bell thought a moment. "Okay, you did great just finding this guy. Let me take care of getting them on board for it."

"What are you going to do? I don't want our grandfathers to know who we are going to see. I want them to think of it as a simple road trip."

"I understand." Bell nodded. "I will enlist my grandmother if I have to, but I think we can get this done."

On Friday that week Jason and Denny were working on the first of the two bikes when Hank came into the shop and sat down. "I guess the women have a destination for the summer bike trip all figured out?"

Jason held his breath and kept working.

"They do?" Denny asked.

"Yeah, they told me this morning that for the summer bike trip they want to go some place they had never been."

"Okay." Denny nodded. "Good idea. Did they say where?"

"Some place named Washington, Louisiana."

"Really? Why there?" Denny asked while Jason tried to keep working while listening.

"They said it just looked like a great little town, and there are tons of things to see on the way there and back." Hank shrugged.

"Okay, where we go doesn't really matter, I suppose." Denny agreed to it. "The big question is when?"

"Well, Bell wants to go, and she will be in Haiti on mission for the last of this month and the first half of July. So how about the first of August."

Denny set his wrench down and looked at Hank a moment. "You realize that the mosquitos down there are not insects as we know them, they are predators and will tear you up."

Hank just laughed. "We will manage somehow. Does repellent help?"

"Yeah, a colt 1911 repellent maybe." Denny replied with a big grin.

For Bell's last day with her Grandparents, they took the boat out to the river and enjoyed a wonderful day fishing and picnicking. Bell surprised everyone by catching the most fish. Several of which were good sized catfish.

The first of Denny's two projects was nearing completion by the end of the next week. That weekend, just the two of them took off on their motorcycles and toured Indiana.

Jason found it amazing that when they rode together, they couldn't say a word, but they shared something just as important, fellowship maybe.

The first bike was completed the next week and the second dismantled. That weekend Hank and Issy invited them to go with them shopping garage sales.

After the fifth stop with many, many more to come, Jason made an observation. "Okay, we go from sale to sale shopping the stuff that people are getting rid of because they have too much stuff. Then we buy it and bring it home to add to the too much stuff we have."

When Bell returned from her mission, she spent a couple of days with her parents and then came to stay at her grandparents so she could be prepared for the long bike trip. Denny had found a couple of backrest bags for the big bikes and a smaller one for Jason's bike.

The week before the trip was spent servicing the bikes and packing. Bell couldn't contain her excitement and that energy rubbed off on the rest of them. The night before setting out Hank cooked burgers on the grill. And while they ate, they made plans for the trip.

By 8AM the next morning the bikes were packed, and they were ready to set out on their adventure. Denny led the way with Jason and Bell right behind and Hank and Issy bringing up the rear.

They headed south on Interstate 69 to Fort Wayne before heading west on Indiana Route 24. It was a beautiful day for riding and the route took them straight across the state, through farming country, small towns and medium to light traffic.

Shortly after crossing the Illinois state line, they headed south on interstate 57 to Champaign then west on Interstate 72 to Springfield. With so much to see and do in Springfield they decided to stop for the night.

The following morning, they visited Lincoln's home, the old State House, the current capitol building, and Lincoln's tomb. From there they headed north to Lincoln's New Salem and spent the balance of the day touring a recreation of the town Lincoln once lived in and ran a store. Finally returning to their hotel and spending another night.

Still in the mood for all things Lincoln, they headed south on 51 to the small town of Vandalia and visited the Old State Capitol. From there they continued south, stopping at the town of West Frankfort and visiting a monument to one of the country's worst coal mine disasters. On December 21, 1951, during the last shift before the holiday break a methane gas explosion ripped through the Orient #2 mine killing 119 miners.

From there they headed south on I-57 until it merged with I-55, then south on I-55 to Memphis. After booking rooms for the night, they visited the Elvis Presley Museum that had just opened a couple of months before. Right across the road from Graceland where the King of Rock and Roll had died almost a year before.

The following morning, they headed southwest on mostly secondary roads stopping only for gas and food. By evening they rolled into the beautiful little town of Washington, Louisiana. As with all stops, the first order of business was to secure rooms for the night, and then find a good place for dinner.

Washington was a beautiful town steeped in history, being the third oldest city in the state of Louisiana. The restaurant was a family affair and offered friendly service and great food. All through dinner Denny and Hank teased Bell about her choice of places for them to travel to.

During the meal, Jason excused himself and went outside to a payphone he had spotted when they pulled up to the restaurant. After a short conversation the plan was all set. Mr. Jenkins suggested that they meet the next morning at the very restaurant they were at.

When they got back to their rooms, Jason secretly told Bell of the plan, who then conveyed it to her grandmother. That turned out to be a necessity as the following morning both Hank and Denny appeared in no hurry to get going.

Finally, it took all three, Jason, Bell, and Issy complaining of being hungry to spur the men along. Mr. Jenkins had told Jason that he would be wearing a ball cap with Army across the front of it so he would recognize him.

As they walked in, Jason spotted Mr. Jenkins at a table with his wife and five empty chairs. Taking the lead, Jason walked right up to the table and asked if the Jenkins would mind if they joined them. At first Denny and Hank both thought the boy had lost his mind.

"That was rude." Denny whispered to Hank.

"Not like it is the only place to sit in here." Hank whispered back noticing several vacant tables they could have sat at.

At the request, both Mr. and Mrs. Jenkins stood up with wide smiles. Mr. Jenkins waved at the empty chairs. "Please, join us."

While everyone was still standing, Jason went ahead with introductions. As soon as he uttered "Sergeant Stanley Jenkins" both Denny and Hank stood transfixed in amazement.

It turned out to be the most wonderful experience, not just for the old war veterans, but for their families as well. After breakfast, Mr. Jenkins gave them a personal tour of his hometown.

That night as they got back to their rooms, both Hank and Denny gave tearful hugs to Jason and Bell for setting it all up.

The trip back home was a totally unplanned adventure. They simply kept heading in a northeast direction and stopping whenever something caught their attention. For a trip that could have been covered in roughly 18 hours, they spent another whole week.

As they were unpacking from the trip Bell joked that they would have to really think on next year's trip if they wanted to out-do this one.

CHAPTER SIXTEEN

Once they got back home, the balance of the summer seemed to race by. Denny and Jason worked on the project bike during the week, and the weekends were spent out on the river with Issy and Hank.

With the school year scheduled to begin right after Labor Day, Jason wanted one last big thing to finish the summer off. He asked Bell if she would like to spend a day with him at the county fair?

"Like a date?" Bell teased.

"Well, yeah. I suppose." Jason felt awkward.

"I'd love that." She laughed. "Are we taking the truck or the bike?"

Jason shrugged. He hadn't thought of that. "Does it matter?"

"Of course, it does." Bell laughed. "I'll have to dress accordingly."

"Gee, I don't care." Jason was at a loss.

"Let's take the truck then." Bell settled the issue. "And pick me up at my house. I'll give you the address."

"Okay." Jason replied.

That night over dinner Jason told his grandfather about the date he had with Bell.

"I'm glad to hear that." Denny smiled. "I like her. I hope the date is a lot of fun for both of you." He then pulled his wallet out and handed Jason some money.

"What's this for?"

"You need money to treat a girl right." Denny laughed. "Besides it is money you've earned helping me in the shop. Now take this and give that sweet girl a night she will remember."

Jason drove the half hour out to the address Bell had given him. Her family lived in a small working community and had a modest home. When Jason knocked on the door, Becky, Bell's mother, answered with a smile and invited him in.

"She'll be down any minute." Becky said, offering him a seat on their sofa.

Five minutes later Bell came down the stairs in a nice pair of slacks, cotton blouse and strap canvas shoes. She had just enough make-up to smooth out the little imperfections in her complexion. Jason thought she was the prettiest girl he had ever met and had a heavenly scent about her as well.

They arrived at the fairground at five and enjoyed exhibits, rides, and more than enough fair food, which both admitted they loved. A pair of necklaces caught Bell's eye and she bought one and Jason bought the other. The necklaces were actually a matched set, with the right half of a heart on one, and the left on the other. Then they placed the necklaces around each other's neck.

For Jason the best part of the day was the ride back to Bell's house. She sat next to him and fell asleep with her head on his shoulder.

When he shut the truck off in her driveway, she awoke feeling embarrassed that she had fallen asleep.

"It's okay." Jason smiled. "I liked having you close. I suppose that proves you feel comfortable with me."

"I really do." Bell smiled. "I also had a great time tonight. Too bad we don't live closer."

"Yeah, that would be nice." Jason said as he got out of the truck and helped her out. From an upstairs window Becky watched Jason and Bell interact and couldn't help but like that young man.

When he got home and was getting ready for bed, he removed his shirt and smelled the shoulder. It made him smile as it smelled like Bell.

His senior year in High School was the busiest of all. He had so many things to do extra. There were colleges to apply to, with Michigan State at the top of his list because of their mechanical engineering program. Senior pictures, S.A.T tests and a whole host of other duties that had to be accomplished.

By the time the senior prom rolled around, he had done all he could do. Michigan State had turned him down. He finally decided that he didn't see any point in spending that kind of money on the first two years anyway. He could attend the local community college at a fraction of the costs, and those credits would transfer.

With the problem of college out of the way, he called Bell and asked if he could stop by to see her.

"I'd like that." Bell laughed.

Right after school, Jason drove out to Bell's house and ended up having to wait over an hour for her to get home. However, her mother Becky enjoyed it, as it gave her a chance to have a cup of coffee and chat with Jason. She would never tell her daughter this, but if she was to pick a boy for Bell, this one would be it.

When Bell got home, and saw Jason's old truck in the drive, she ran into the house.

"I am sorry I'm late." Bell explained. "I got tied up with a yearbook problem that we had to solve."

"It's okay, really." Jason said to calm her.

"No problem honey." Becky laughed. "I was just telling Jason what a handful you can be."

"MOM!"

Jason laughed. "She didn't." Then he thought for a moment. "Should she have?"

Bell gave him that look he had learned to read so well. The look of, how could you?

Jason gave Bell a hug and said how nice it was to see her.

"Thank you. You too." Bell smiled sweetly. "You came all the way out just to see me?"

"Well, partly." Jason blushed a little. "That and to ask a favor of you."

Bell's heart skipped a beat, being the time of year that it was, she kind of felt she knew what that favor would be. "What can I do for you?"

"My senior prom is in a couple of weeks, and I was wondering if you would honor me by being my date for that?"

Becky had been standing around the corner and listening. When she heard Jason ask Bell to the prom, she smiled to herself and then walked away.

"Oh, I would love to go." Bell gushed. "I was hoping that you would ask. What night is it?"

"The 19th." Jason was so happy she said yes. Now, suddenly worried that the date would be an issue.

"That's perfect!" Bell replied. "On one condition."

"Which is?"

"Mine is on the 26th." Bell replied. "I will go with you to yours if you will take me to mine."

Jason laughed and wrapped his arms around her. "I would love to."

The proms were something special to both. Jason and Bell felt really close to each other and realized that they had very strong feelings toward one another.

A week before graduation, Jason received a letter from a small prestigious college not far from his home. It offered a special rate and a couple of scholarships for students entering the engineering field. Room and board were also included in the deal, so he felt he couldn't turn it down. He had simply not even considered Olivet College before.

Before accepting, however, he talked it over with his grandfather.

"That is a highly thought of school." Denny said, after Jason explained it all to him. "Plus, it isn't that far from home, so you can come home on the weekends."

"You gonna be okay with me gone?"

Denny sat and thought for a moment and then nodded. "Yeah, I'll be just fine. I would appreciate it if you give me a few cooking lessons though."

The stewardess had turned the overhead lights down low, and most of the passengers were sleeping. He pulled the small chain around his neck and pulled it out from under his shirt. It still held the half-heart after all this time. Bell had given it to him. She had a similar one around her neck back then with the other half of the heart attached to hers.

Going to Olivet had certainly opened doors for him. He got lucky in his roommate in the dorm, John. Through his friendship with John, he met Phillip, which led him to his career. Staring out the window into the pitch-dark night, he thought of how lucky he was. He did, however, consider what his luck had cost him. In the ten years since he left for college, he had never spent more than a couple of weeks with his grandfather. At first that wasn't much of a concern. But the last two or three trips back home reminded him that grandfather was very mortal. He had aged more each time. He was always so glad to see Jason, and even got teary-eyed when it was time for Jason to leave.

The biggest cost of taking a job so far from home hit him especially hard when grandfather called and told him that Hank had passed away.

Jason remembered flying home for the visitation and funeral. Grandfather asked Jason to drive to the visitation, since he didn't drive anymore than he had to. Jason had to smile when they made their way out to the garage.

Grandfather still had the old car, and the 1957 Ford pickup. They decided to take the pickup for old-time's sake.

By this time grandfather was already having to walk with a cane, and it was a bit tough for him to get into the higher cab, but with Jason's help he got there.

They had to walk about half a block to get to the funeral home and then wait in line to speak to the family. As they passed the casket and looked down on their old friend, he looked good, at peace. Before walking away from the casket, Denny came to attention and saluted his friend. It was when they got to the family that Jason had to check his emotions. After giving Bell a hug and saying how sorry he was, she introduced him to William, her boyfriend.

Jason kept staring out into the vastness of black space as he thought of Bell. He held the heart necklace tighter and realized the true cost of taking the job with Phillip. Then he realized that there was nothing to be done about it now. Bell had probably married that fellow and had children by now.

After speaking to and hugging Becky, and shaking Bell's dad's hand, he came to Issy. Issy looked much older then and more fragile. She was sitting on one of those walker/chair type things and thanking the people that had come to pay respects.

When Jason stepped in front of her, Issy burst into tears and held her arms out to him for a hug. Jason bent down and took her in his arms and held her tight as she cried. When she released her grip on him, Jason stood back up, tears in his own eyes.

"Please pull one of those chairs over here and sit with me, would you?" Issy pleaded. Becky heard her mother and slipped out of line and pulled a chair for Jason next to her mom. Jason nodded his thanks and noticed the tears in Becky's eyes as well.

Denny pulled a chair up behind them but stayed far enough back so not to intrude. Issy held Jason's hand and kept telling him how proud she was of him, and how happy it made her to see him again. None of which passed Becky's or Bell's attention, or William's for that matter.

Jason stayed with her and they talked between her need to thank the people that came. Issy told him that she was so sure he would come that she listed him as a pallbearer.

As luck would have it, Jason's position at the side of the casket was directly across from William. After the burial Jason also sat with Issy and attended to her needs by getting a plate of food for her and a drink.

Several times Jason and Bell exchanged glances, but it wasn't until it was time to leave, that Bell gave Jason a hug and told him how good it was to see him.

Jason visited with Issy in her home several times before having to catch the flight back to his new home and job.

He had made a couple of trips back home to see Grandfather, and of course Issy, but he didn't see Bell or her parents either time. Each time he went back, he was aware of how much grandfather and Issy were aging. Both were having more trouble getting around and both had gotten some in-home care. Ladies that would come in twice a week and help clean, shop, and do laundry for them.

CHAPTER SEVENTEEN

In the distance Jason could see the lights of a city, and then another and another. As the jet flew over Chicago the ground was ablaze with lights. Shortly after Chicago the fasten seat belt sign came on with a light alert tone.

As the plane touched down and then taxied to the terminal the pilot came on the speaker and welcomed the passengers to Detroit. The weather was a crisp forty-six degrees. The rental car agent had his paperwork ready and before his luggage hit the carousel, he had the keys in his pocket.

The car he had rented was a bit harder to find. It was described as a white Buick, of which there happened to be a fleet of white cars, half of which were Buicks.

On the drive from Detroit, he debated whether he should just get a room for the night, or just go to grandfather's house. He worried that he might wake grandfather, but also was a bit concerned that if he didn't go home and grandfather passed, could he forgive himself? He decided to just go home.

He had expected the call, but it hurt when it came. Was he going home for the last time? Would he get home in time?

It had been a four-hour flight and he lost a few hours crossing time zones. It would be the middle of the night by the time he got to the house.

Denny was in a hospital bed located in front of the living room window to give him a view of the world he was about to leave. He had been asleep until the headlights of a car pulling into the driveway woke him. He smiled as he watched Jason get out of the car and make his way to the front door.

Jason had figured that he would arrive about this time, so he had brought along his house key, the same key he been carrying for more than a decade. He entered the house as quietly as he could and had just relocked the front door when a light suddenly snapped on.

He turned and saw that the light was next to a hospital bed by the bay window. His grandfather had seen him come in.

"Welcome home." Denny rasped out.

"Thank you. It is good to be here." Jason replied quietly. "I just wish you felt better."

Denny put a finger to his lips to signal Jason to speak quietly, then motioned toward the sofa. Jason noticed a lady was sleeping on it.

"I am doing okay, all things considered." Denny forced a grin. "Much better now that you are here."

Jason set his overnight bag down and went into the dining room and grabbed a chair. Sitting down next to his grandfather, he reached out and took his hand. For the longest time they didn't say anything, just held each other's hand.

"Who called you?" Denny asked.

"The hospice office." Jason replied.

"Guess the end is near then."

"Don't say that." Jason started to tear up. "I still need you."

Denny squeezed his hand. "There might have been a time that that was true, not anymore. You have made me very proud."

"Thank you."

They talked for over an hour before Denny was just too tired. Jason fell asleep in the chair next to grandfather's bed. He awoke to the smell of fresh coffee brewing. Jason got up and stretched, the chair had really kinked his body. He stepped from the living room into the kitchen and felt his heart drop.

The nurse had her back to him, but there was no mistaking that red hair. Just as he was about to speak, she turned around, and not knowing he was behind her, she jumped in surprise.

"Good morning, Jason." Bell smiled sweetly. "I thought that might be your car in the drive. What time did you get in?"

"Good morning, Bell." Jason had to find his voice. He hadn't seen her since her grandfather's funeral. She had filled out some and her smile made her the most beautiful girl he had ever seen. "I got here in the middle of the night. Had a nice visit with grandfather before we both fell asleep."

"Aww." Bell titled her head just so, which made her eyes seem brighter. "I am so glad you were able to get here. He really was praying that he would get to see you again."

"I didn't know you were his nurse." Jason said. "He didn't tell me that, nor was it you on the phone yesterday."

"I had the office call you." She replied, and then smiled. "And asked your grandfather to keep that a secret between us."

"William okay with you being here?" Jason didn't know how else to broach the subject. He hadn't noticed a ring, but often nurses don't wear them during work.

"Who?" Bell was confused.

"William." Jason repeated. "Your boyfriend or maybe now your..."

Bell laughed. "Oh, my goodness! I haven't seen him since a few weeks after Grandpa Hank's funeral. He wasn't thrilled with my families' response to you."

"What?"

"Oh, he noticed." Bell laughed, grabbing a couple of coffee mugs out of the cupboard.

"He noticed what?"

"First, my reaction to seeing you." Bell answered as she poured out two cups, then added sugar to hers. "You want sugar and cream?"

"No, black."

"Ick!" Bell laughed as she handed Jason the one cup and doctored hers. Then she peeked around the corner to be sure Denny was still asleep. Then she took Jason by the hand and led him out to the front porch and a couple of chairs there.

After they sat down, Bell took a sip of her coffee before continuing. "He wasn't happy with what he saw between us, but when he saw how my parents reacted to you, that made it worse. Then when grandma saw you and reacted the way she did, I think he finally understood where he stood with my family."

"Your family has always been good to me." Jason admitted. "Especially your grandmother. She was there when I needed her most. Thanks to her, the relationship between my grandfather and myself did a complete about-face."

"Her love of you went way beyond that." Bell commented. "She always asks me about you, as if she thinks we have kept in touch."

Jason just smiled. "Maybe she was nudging you to call me."

"Maybe." Bell conceded. "But you could have called me too."

"Well, maybe." Jason replied. "I guess after meeting William, I figured I was too late. Maybe, if I had known the truth, I probably would have."

"Really?" Bell smiled that sweet smile that tugged at Jason's heart.

"I have thought of you so often over the years." Jason admitted. "Just last night on the flight I thought about everything I gave up taking the job out west. You were at the top of that list."

A tear fell down Bell's cheek. "Really?"

Jason didn't answer. Instead, he reached for the thin necklace around his neck and pulled the half of a heart out into view.

Bell started to openly cry. She pulled the matching necklace out from under her top and held it out to Jason. He reached over and placed his heart with hers, making it a complete heart for the first time in a decade.

Bell was emotionally blown away and crying harder, so Jason moved over next to her and took her in his arms and held her tight.

What neither of them knew was that Denny had awakened and was watching them through the window, and he wasn't the only one. Across the lawn tears were also falling down Issy's cheeks.

When Bell finally got control of her emotions, she glanced over at the bay window and noticed that Denny was awake. Still in Jason's arms, she looked up and smiled. "We have an audience, and it is time for me to get to work."

Jason bent down and planted a quick kiss on her tear covered lips. "Need a hand?"

"I'd love that." Bell replied while walking to the front door. "So would your grandfather."

When they stepped into the living room, Denny was smiling and watching them come over to him. "That sight was the best thing to wake up to."

"What sight was that?" Jason asked, playing innocent.

Denny just gave him that look that Jason had learned to read over the years. "You two together."

Bell smiled, but then stepped into her role as his nurse. "Denny, do you need to go to the Throne room?"

Hearing her use Denny's pet name for the bathroom made Jason smile.

"I do." Denny replied, while weakly throwing the covers off himself. Bell went and grabbed the wheelchair and moved it in close to the bed.

“Give me a hand.” Bell told Jason. Which he did. Once they had Denny in the wheelchair, Bell asked Jason to bring along the crutches.

Watching Denny get himself into the Throne Room brought back a lot of memories. Once he reached a point that he could manage on his own, Bell stepped back and closed the door.

When Denny had taken care of business, Bell reminded him that he needed to get cleaned up that day.

“Let me help him do that.” Jason offered.

“You sure?” Bell asked.

“Be like old times.” Denny forced a half laugh. Which made Jason smile.

While Jason was helping his grandfather bathe as best he could, Bell went into the bedroom and retrieved clean underwear and pajamas. A hospital gown would make things a lot easier, but Denny wouldn’t have it.

Then to Bell’s surprise, instead of helping Denny back to his bed, Jason got him out to the dining-room table and helped him transfer to what had been his place at the head of the table.

“A Grandmother Judy breakfast?” Jason asked.

"I have dreamed of it." Denny nodded.

Jason went out into the kitchen and found none of the things he needed, so he instantly remembered Issy's phone number and gave her a call.

"Hello?" Issy answered.

"Grandma Issy, I want to make grandfather a good breakfast, but he doesn't have anything to do it with."

"Jason?" Issy acted surprised, even though she had watched him and Bell on the porch.

"It's me." Jason laughed.

"What do you need honey."

"Eggs, bacon, and potatoes." Jason replied. "He has bread for toast."

"Oh, I am sorry, I don't have any bacon, and only a couple of eggs, but I'll let you have them." Issy replied.

"Don't worry then." Jason said. "I will make a quick trip to the store, but I am going to be cooking enough for four, so if you would honor us with your presence, say in about half an hour, I would appreciate that."

Why thank you." Issy answered. "I can come over very soon. I do have a favor to ask of you."

"What can I do for you." Jason asked.

"I need a few things from the store as well. If I make a short list, and then come over and be with your grandfather, could Bell go with you to get my things?"

"If it is okay with Bell, that would be fine with me."

"If what would be okay with me?" Bell asked as Jason hung up the phone.

"I need to run to the store for supplies for here, and your grandmother needs some things too. She is coming over to sit with grandfather if you will go with me to get the things she needs." Jason explained.

Bell looked at Jason a moment with that look of hers. "Fine."

"What?" Jason was at a loss.

"That will be fine." Bell said as she turned away and went back to stripping the bedding from the hospital bed.

Once Issy was there and Jason and Bell were in his rental car, Jason looked at her. "Okay, what was that look you gave me?"

Bell laughed. "You sure don't understand women."

"What's that supposed to mean?"

Bell was still smiling and shaking her head. "If you looked in my grandmother's panty, you would see enough food to feed an army. This list she gave me has not one essential item on it."

"I don't understand." Jason admitted.

Bell reached over and patted Jason's arm. "My grandmother just wanted us to spend a little time together. She doesn't need any of these things, at least not right now."

Jason looked over at her. "And the downside is what?"

Bell burst into laughter. "Start the car Mr. Wood. Your grandfather can't sit in that wooden chair forever."

At the store Bell had gathered up all the items on her list while Jason was still in the second aisle. His cart had several items, but not one complete meal. Bell took charge and helped him figure out enough meals for a week, while cautioning him on the kinds of things his grandfather shouldn't be eating.

Jason loaded both carts onto the belt and paid for everything himself. Once they had everything loaded in the trunk and were back in the car Bell said something about that.

"Grandma gave me money for her things."

Jason just looked over at her. "Then do what you just told me women are so good at. Give it back to her without her knowing it."

Bell just laughed and sat there watching him drive. When they were about half of the way home, she broke the silence. "What are you thinking?"

"Right now?"

"No last Thursday! Of course, right now."

Jason glanced over at her. "I was just thinking that this little trip was the most enjoyable trip to a grocery store I have ever had."

Bell smiled and tilted her head slightly which had her long red hair spill across her face. She brushed the hair aside and flashed those bright blue eyes at him. Jason suddenly realized that once again God had answered a prayer.

Of course, Bell quickly killed that tender moment. "So, you like that store huh?"

Jason just gave her a stern look, which made her laugh.

They were both laughing when they came through the front door. Issy looked at Denny and winked, which made him smile.

CHAPTER EIGHTEEN

While Jason made breakfast, Bell finished making Denny's bed, and then loaded the washing machine and got the laundry started.

Then she set the place settings up and got coffee for everyone. She knew grandma liked hers with lots of cream and a little sugar, which she made just right. Denny was like his Grandson; he liked his coffee black. When Jason brought the food to the table, they all joined hands for a very rare treat; his grandfather said the prayer. He gave thanks for all the blessings he had received. His grandson coming home, having the best neighbor a man could ask for, and the most attentive, attractive, and available nurse.

When Denny said that Issy squeezed Bell's hand at the exact moment Jason squeezed her other hand. It was all Bell could do to keep from laughing.

After a wonderful meal together, Denny was exhausted; and Jason and Bell helped him back into bed. Issy hugged them both and headed across the lawn to her house. First, she told Bell that instead of driving home, she should just stay with her for a while.

Bell accepted the offer and when she called her mother to explain, the first response from her mother was, "Jason back home?"

"Yes, mom. He is."

Jason made a fresh pot of coffee and the two of them went out on the front porch, where they could keep an eye on Denny, should he need them.

"I was just thinking back to when we were kids." Jason said. "I wanted to become an industrial Engineer, and you wanted to be a nurse."

"We did it, didn't we?" Bell smiled. "Although I was torn between being a nurse and a missionary."

"What helped you decide?"

"I did a couple of missions right here in the US." Bell replied. "Your grandfather went on one of those with me."

"Yeah," Jason nodded. "He told me about that over the phone when he got home. He enjoyed it. Said it was about fixing up old homes for the poor."

"It was." Bell replied. "Your grandfather was amazing at getting what had to be done, done."

"That was gramps." Jason laughed.

"Where you get it from too." Bell teased. "Anyway, it was during those last two missions that I realized that there was much to be done right here at home. In my first year of college, I worked part time in assisted home care. I loved it. I realized that I could fulfill my dreams right here at home. Make a difference in my own community."

"I wish I had found that." Jason frowned.

"Did you even look?" Bell asked with a bit of an edge to her voice.

Jason caught the tone and looked her in the eyes for a moment. "No, I guess I didn't. I felt honored by what Phillip was offering me and just took it. Job and pay wise, it was a great opportunity."

"Grandfather Hank always said that life was a trade-off." Bell sighed. "Have you ever wondered what your life would have been if you had found work close to home?"

"Often." Jason replied. "I guess more so as I got older."

"Oh?" Bell asked. "What do you think would have been different?"

"A lot of things." Jason admitted. "Probably some bad with the good, like your grandfather always said."

"Like what bad things?"

"Well, for one I probably wouldn't be making the kind of money I am now. I would probably still be living right here in this house and wonder if that would have become a factor in my relationship with Grandpa."

"Why would that have been a factor in your relationship?" Bell asked.

"I don't know." Jason replied. "Is still living with your parents a problem?"

"Oh, but I don't." Bell answered. "I bought the house next door to them. With their help of course."

"Really?"

"Yes, really." Bell nodded. "I can't imagine living so far away from my family like you do."

"There are pros and cons." Jason said. "The good side of it, is you come and go as you like, no unspoken expectations. The downside is that you are alone."

Bell just looked at him with a sad understanding look. "Sometimes you can be surrounded by family and still feel alone."

"Your grandmother told me that once too."

"What did you miss most about home while living out there?" Bell asked.

"Different things would come to mind from time to time." Jason admitted. "One thing always seemed to do so a lot more than others though."

"What was that?"

Jason looked her in the eyes. "You."

"Me? Then why didn't you ever call me?" Bell's eyes started getting moist.

"I just figured that by then you would have found someone. Gotten married and had a family." Jason replied. "In fact, I am still amazed that you didn't. Besides, you never called me either."

Bell turned away from him as a tear fell. Looking out across the lawn toward her grandmother's house, and then slowly back at Jason. "I suppose for the same reasons you didn't call me. Although, I had been given that suggestion numerous times by my parents, and of course grandma. I dated guys from time to time, it just never felt right. I never felt that... well, you know."

Jason smiled. "Yes, I do know. I dated as well. They just never seemed to measure up."

"Measure up to what?"

"You." Jason looked her in the eyes. "Almost from the moment I met you, I always had this feeling inside that I understood you and felt you did me as well. I was always naturally comfortable when we were together. I just never found that with another. I guess, I just never felt like I was just me when with any other girl."

The tears were flowing down Bell's face.

Jason got up out of his chair and knelt in front of her. "Would you give me another chance?"

Bell was out of her chair and in his arms almost before the words had left his lips followed by the long passionate kiss that both had waited years for.

Tears were running down Issy's cheeks as well as she dialed her daughter's phone number to let her know that their prayers just might be getting answered.

After the kiss, Jason looked into Bell's teary eyes. "Would you like to start with a date tonight?"

"I would love that." Bell smiled. "It'll be late because we will have to wait for the night nurse to get here."

"I don't care if it is midnight." Jason assured her.

Jason made supper for grandfather, while Bell ran over to her grandmother's, to freshen up. While Denny was eating, he kept looking at Jason. He noticed something about him but couldn't put a finger on it.

"You know," Denny finally spoke. "When the night nurse gets here, you should get out, take some time off."

Jason laughed. "I've only been here a day grandpa."

Denny thought about that for a moment. "Even so, I bet Bell would like a night out."

Jason laughed out loud. "Is there a conspiracy here?"

"What? What do you mean?" Denny asked.

"With you and Bell's family? You all seem to be nudging us along."

Denny looked at Jason for a moment. "Son, we are only encouraging what we know is truth. Her family and I saw it in you two from the moment you met. On the motorcycle trips you two were always close, and we could plainly see that you both liked it that way. And from what I saw of you two on the porch this afternoon that hasn't changed."

"I thought you were sleeping." Jason noted.

"Of course, I was." Denny laughed.

Issy thought waiting for the night nurse to arrive before their date was plain silly. She insisted on staying with Denny until that happened.

For starters, they went to the old family style restaurant that they had always gone to as kids. It had changed hands and was no longer as clean or as good.

"Well, not everything stands the test of time." Jason joked as they walked out to his car.

Bell snuggled up under his arm. "The important things do."

They drove down to the city park and walked down along the river, finally settling on a park bench facing the river.

They talked about many things, one of which was how important this old river had been to them growing up. The pontoon boat that her grandparents had bought. Issy's faded red bandana, and how it had opened Denny's and Jason's eyes to faith. Then they just sat in silence, hand in hand.

Jason then pulled her hand up and kissed it. "I am so amazed by you." He told her. "Being with you is so natural, so comforting, and so easy. I feel just the same with you as I did when we were kids."

Bell smiled. "I was just thinking the same thing. I love being with you. I can say anything and not have it judged or interpreted for hidden meaning. I also feel a gentle tenderness, a feeling of belonging. A true feeling of being loved and in love."

Jason cupped her face with his hands and tenderly kissed her lips. "I do love you, Bell. I always have and always will."

The moment they admitted their love, Jason slid off the bench to his knees before her. He reached into his pocket and pulled his grandmother's ring out and proposed to her.

The ring would have to be sized down to Bell's finger size, but she tearfully accepted the proposal. After a tight embrace and kiss, they just stared into each other's eyes.

"Do you want a big wedding?" Jason asked.

"Mister Wood, I would accept exchanging vows with you in a dark alley conducted by a drunken Justice of the Peace."

"When would you like to get married?" Jason asked.

"What are you doing tomorrow?" Bell laughed. Which planted a seed in Jason's mind. He sat Bell back down on the bench and took her hand as he sat next to her and explained what he had in mind. She loved it.

CHAPTER NINETEEN

Neither Jason nor Bell would explain why, but they asked her parents and grandmother, and Denny to a formal dinner they were planning for that Saturday afternoon.

There were questions to be sure, but when the kids weren't forthcoming, they accepted it. Of course, everyone was pretty sure of the reason. The kids were going to announce their engagement.

Bell asked Issy if she would mind watching Denny while she and Jason ran a few errands. To justify what they had told Denny and Issy, they did stop at the grocery store and got the supplies for the feast on Saturday.

At noon on Saturday Bell's parents arrived at Issy's and walked her over to Denny's. Jason had Denny all dressed up in his best suit. Unbeknown to Issy, is that Bell had gotten Issy's wedding dress out of her closet and had it altered slightly and dry cleaned.

When Bell opened the front door and led them in, Issy recognized the dress immediately.

"That's my old wedding dress!"

"Yes, it is," Bell smiled and took her grandmother's arm and led her to the end of the end table opposite Denny.

Jason was in the kitchen in his shirt sleeves getting everything into serving dishes.

All through dinner, Jason and Bell kept skirting the questions. Finally, Bell's father couldn't stand the suspense any longer.

"Okay, this has been truly wonderful, and we are grateful. We think we know what this is all about, so why don't you just announce it."

"Soon daddy," Bell giggled. "Just be patient."

No sooner had Bell said that, than the front doorbell rang. Jason jumped out of his chair and went to the door. A moment later he came back into the dining room with a guest. "Everyone, I would like to introduce you to Reverend Plock."

No one knew what to say, other than stand and greet the minister.

Bell stepped over to Jason's side and he pulled his jacket back on. "Mom, Dad, grandma, and Mr. Wood. Reverend Plock is here to conduct a little service that

Jason and I would like you to be a part of."

The other four people quickly exchanged surprised glances.

"Grandfather, Mr. Barnes." Jason addressed the two men. I would like to have you both serve me as Men of Honor with you Grandpa as my best man, which you have always been."

Before they could answer, Bell spoke. "Grandma Issy and mom, I would like to ask the same of you both. And since grandma is responsible for my first meeting of Jason, I would like you to be my matron of Honor."

They were speechless. Bell's father was the first to find his voice. "You're getting married? Like right now?"

"Yes sir." Jason replied. "Bell and I have both learned the cost of putting things off and should have done this years ago."

"You going to get married in here?" Denny asked."

"Well, we were thinking in the back yard under the big Maple. If that's okay?"

While everyone got their jackets on, and make-up touched up. The minister went out to his car and brought his wife back. She was an avid photographer and had brought her camera. Jason first put the engagement ring on Bell's finger and then handed the wedding band to Denny. As Denny looked down at the ring, he recognized it instantly and looked up at Jason with tears in his eyes.

"Is using her rings, okay?" Jason asked. Knowing he should have asked before, but that would have blown the surprise.

Denny was choked up and couldn't reply, but enthusiastically nodded his head.

The service was as beautiful as it was simple, all Jason and Bell had ever dreamed of. The only dry eyes amongst them were the minister and his wife.

After the service, the minister had them sign the license and gave them a copy. They had planned on cleaning the kitchen and dining room before the night nurse got there and then just going to Bell's house for their wedding night.

The others wouldn't hear of it. They insisted that they take a honeymoon. Issy and Becky would help Denny until they got back home in a week or so.

"We hadn't planned on that." Bell thanked them. "We don't even know where we would go."

"It's not the destination little girl." Denny replied. "It's the company."

Bell looked at Jason as he winked and turned to his grandfather. "Could I then ask another favor?"

"You can." Denny answered, knowing what was going through Jason's mind. "Want to do a bike honeymoon?"

Bell's eyes lit up when she heard that.

"May we borrow the bike and sidecar that we built?"

"You can." Denny replied. "But it hasn't been ridden in a few years. It needs to be serviced. All the gas drained out and fresh gas installed. Oil changed, and a new battery."

Jason smiled. "That won't take that long to do. I'll change clothes and go get the gas, oil and battery out of it now. Then run into town and get the supplies."

Bell's dad helped get the bike ready to go, while Bell went with her mother and grandmother back to Issy's house. Bell changed into comfortable riding clothes, and then very carefully hung grandma's wedding dress back in her closet.

South Haven was as far as they got that night. Their first night as a married couple was tender, loving, and memorable. The rest of their honeymoon was spent retracing the first bike tour they took as kids together.

When they got back home, Issy commented on the glow of love about Bell. Waiting for Jason was a call from Phillip. Jason returned the call and the two of them talked for over two hours.

When Phillip had first called and was told that Jason was away on his honeymoon, he knew from conversations in the past with Jason who he had married. A part of him was happy, as he considered Jason a son. Then he was concerned that he might have just lost his best design engineer.

Over the phone, they came up with a plan. The broken or worn-out parts would be shipped right to Jason in Michigan. He could then draft the plans for re-creating those parts and then overnight those plans to Phillip.

For the next six months, Denny seemed to be doing better. Several times, Jason and Bell rented a pontoon boat and took Issy and Denny out on the river. By this time Bell was very pregnant. From what the doctor told her; she had conceived on their honeymoon.

During a snowstorm in late January Bell went into labor. Jason got her to their car, put the luggage in the trunk, and then helped Denny and Issy get into the back seat. This was something neither wanted to miss and had made the kids promise they could be there for it.

Bell had called her parents when the labor pains started, and they were already at the hospital by the time Jason got everyone there.

At 1AM Denton Henry Wood came into the world. Jason, Issy, and Becky were all in the delivery room to witness the entire thing. While the nurse cleaned little Denny up, Jason glanced out the window and for a moment watched the snow falling. He thought back to a night very much like this when he lost his parents. Now a new life, and a new chapter in his life began on just such a night.

By the time the nurse had the baby cleaned and nursing, Bell had passed the placenta. The nurse then took a few minutes to clean Bell, before covering her and allowing Bell's father and Denny into the room.

Seeing his grandfather holding the baby, with happy tears, made Jason tear up as well. They would never be able to get a four generations picture, but he couldn't help but feel that his parents and Grandma Judy were in the room with them.

Three months later Denny started getting very weak. He lingered for a week, spending his awake moments with Jason and talking. The last thing Denny said to Jason was whispered as he held Jason's hand. "Thank you, son. Thank you for being there when I lost my only reasons for living. Thank you for being there for me, for giving me new reasons for living. For bringing pleasure to my empty life. For giving me a life worth living. And above all, for helping me find Jesus, because of that when I do get to go home, I will be with your dad and my Judy again."

After his death Denny's ashes were mixed with Grandma Judy's and then interred next to his parent's graves. Issy would live long enough to see three more babies come into the world.

Bell's parents spoiled the children as Jason imagined his parents would have done, but it was Issy that was completely under the children's control. Anything they wanted, Issy got for them.

After Issy passed, Bell's father and Jason remodeled Hank and Issy's house so as soon as he retired, grandpa and grandma Barnes would move in next door.

Made in the USA
Monee, IL
20 November 2023

46872435R00163